Timeless

Phoebe Smythe

Published by Phoebe Smythe, 2024.

TIMELESS

First edition. May 15, 2024.

ISBN: 979-8224803798

Written by Phoebe Smythe.

Dedicated to those who remind me of music.

Prologue

Time After Time – Cyndi Lauper

Saturday, 10th June 2023

A man strolled along the bridge, absorbing his surroundings with a keen eye. Towering palm trees dotted the southern bank, their lush leaves casting dappled shadows on the sunlit path. The gentle murmur of Ballona Creek flowed beneath the bridge, weaving a tranquil melody through nature. Cyndi Lauper's music blared in his headphones, but his attention was drawn to the details around him: the pale buildings with their intricately carved windows, the fences blocking off the rocky terrain, and a girl in the water. His heart quickened with a flicker of unease, and he moved towards the water to get a closer look.

"Shit!" His heart thudded, and the calm that enveloped his summer holiday shattered. He ignored the fencing, ripped his headphones down to his shoulders, and scrambled down the jagged rocks. His eyes wide and his pulse fast, he reached the girl's side, quickly moving her into the recovery position. He ripped his phone out his pocket, his lips parting as he dialled 911, speaking with a ragged voice.

"There's a girl in the water near Ballona Creek Bridge. I'm with her now. She looks lifeless and she's freezing. I don't know how long she's been here for. Please help."

"We'll be about 15 minutes. Put her in the recovery position. Can you do CPR?"

"Yes." Time seemed to stretch, as he placed the heels of his hands into the middle of her chest, and pushed down.

Chapter One

Forever Young– Bob Dylan

"Check blood pressure and oxygen saturation, stat!"

"120 over 80. Oxygen saturation at 95. She's stable," reported a nurse, her tone both reassuring and attentive.

In the sterile hospital room, the urgent commands echoed, punctuating the air like a call to action. The girl stirred, her eyes fluttering open, trying to make sense of the unfamiliar surroundings. As harsh lights bore down on her, she squinted, her dry lips parting as she reached for the cannula in her nose.

"Miss, can you hear me? What's your name?" The nurse's voice was gentle but firm, cutting through the confusion. A fog of confusion clouded her eyes as she tried to grasp her surroundings. "Josephine Melrose," she managed to utter, her voice weak and trembling, as she struggled to sit up. "Where am I? What happened? What's the date?"

"You're at a hospital in Los Angeles, California," the nurse replied, her voice soothing. She gestured toward the man sitting beside the bed, his eyes wide with concern and curiosity. "This is August Quinn. He found you unconscious at Ballona Creek. It's June 10th 2023."

"2023!?" Josephine's brows shot up as her wide eyes darted around the room, struggling to piece together the fragments of her memory. She nodded slowly and attempted to sit up, her gaze locking with August's.

"I'm going to go and take a look at your file, Miss Melrose. Will you be okay?" Josephine nodded and watched the room empty. Everyone except August left. He sat on the mattress and offered a tentative smile and wave. "Hey, I'm August," he said softly, offering a gentle smile, "You had us worried back there."

"I'm Josie. What is this beeping thing?"

He tapped the side of the machine, "It's an electrocardiogram, ECG. It tracks your heart's rhythm."

Confusion painted her features, and she tilted her head, placing a hand on her chest. "M-my heart?"

"Have you never seen a medical show before?" August asked, a mix of amusement and surprise evident in his voice.

"A show?"

"On television," August clarified gently, sensing her lack of familiarity with modern technology. "Are you even in the 21st century?"

"Hm?" She shook her head slightly. "I-I don't know." The worlds they inhabited seemed worlds apart, yet there was a hint of curiosity in her gaze. Their conversation was interrupted as a doctor reentered the room, her eyes wide and face pale as she clutched helplessly on a worn clipboard. August sat back, watching Josephine's expression closely as the doctor's words unfolded.

"Miss Melrose, we can't find any records for you after 1912. It says you died aged eighteen in the sinking of *Titanic*."

Her eyes widened, and her hands drifting to her mouth, her eyes flicking over to August's whose eyebrows were raised. The revelation hit her like a tidal wave, and her heart pounded in her chest. 1912? *Titanic*? She swallowed, trying to rid the lump in her throat. August's face blanched, and he gripped the bed sheets. She shuddered, seeing the ship in her mind again, watching as she tumbled down the side of it. She locked eyes with him, trying to see or hear anything but the dying ship in her mind. Her mind pushed her underwater, and she gasped for air, her eyes stinging as she searched the room for anything to stop the memories.

"Well I think it's impossible. That'd make her..."

"129 years old," August finished, awe and wonder in his tone as he struggled to comprehend the enigmatic figure before him. "Damn, that's impressive, Josie. Are you a time traveller or something?"

"No." The doctor dismissed. "It must be a typo."

"Either that or she's got Chrono Eternal Anomaly Syndrome."

"CEAS?" Another nurse whispered. "But that's just a— only 2% of the population have it."

"Is it even possible?"

The doctor hesitated, her professional demeanour faltering for a moment. "I-In theory, yes. But it's so rarely documented."

August leaned forward, his eyes narrow. "So what does this mean for Josie?"

The doctor sighed, her shoulders slumping slightly. "It means we have a lot of questions to answer. And a lot of research to do."

Josie swallowed hard, her mind racing with the implications of her newfound diagnosis. "No—"

"Well other than the whole CEAS thing, you're actually really healthy, Miss Melrose. "Your vitals are stable, and there's no sign of secondary drowning, which is good news as this condition is known to cause a weakened immune system. If you're feeling well enough, we can discharge you and provide support to help you reintegrate back home."

"No! I don't want to be someone's pet project! And I can't go back home, you eejits!"

"Hey, hey, it's okay," he whispered, taking her hand. "Where's home?"

"Belfast." she breathed, and he scratched the nape of his neck.

"Listen, it's a long stretch, but if you like, you can stay with me," he stroked her hand gently. "We'll figure it out together."

She managed a small smile, her heart now tethered to this newfound connection. She nodded slowly, pensively. "Thank you, August."

"I just need you both to sign the discharge papers and we'll let you both go."

Josie smiled at August, dumbfounded by the new world around her. He smiled back, taking her hand. The nurse handed her a clipboard and a pen.

"Just sign your name here. We've washed and dried your clothes and you can use the washroom to change."

Josephine Éabha Melrose

"And you, sir."

August Milo Quinn

Josie stood up, a wave of vertigo washing over her body as she stumbled towards a small room. Minutes later she emerged with her gown neatly folded and handed it to the nurse, before taking August's hand and flashing a soft smile. "Come on, I've got to show you everything you've missed."

Chapter Two

Counting Stars – OneRepublic

"So, did you freeze to death or did you hit a propeller blade or something?" August swung her arm as they walked down the hospital corridor, his curiosity getting the best of him. "Well obviously not completely to death because you're here but— sorry, that was insensitive. You don't speak much, do you?"

She smiled sadly. "I don't really know what to say to you."

"Well can we start by how a girl managed to travel over a century into the future without a clue how she got here."

She cocked her head, raising an eyebrow as she held back a smile. "You just answered yourself, August." Josie smiled coyly, watching his eyebrows thread together. "I don't know how I got here."

"Well I suppose I'll have to become a detective then."

"Really?"

He shrugged. "If it means getting to know you better, then yes."

Her eyes sparkled, as her mouth widened into a grin. "You want to become a detective just to know more about me?"

He nodded, a small smile playing on his lips, and her eyes widened. "Yes, I do. Obviously it's not every day that someone from the past shows up in our time. You're fascinating, and I want to get to know you."

She looked away for a moment, losing herself in a thought. "It's not as exciting as you might think. I'm quite scared."

August placed a hand on her shoulder, watching her eyes. "I bet you are. It must be overwhelming. But we'll figure this out together, I promise. I won't leave you to figure it out on your own."

He pushed open the glass door which led to a busy road. Cars zoomed past in blurs, droning across the tarmac. Josie stood frozen for a moment, her eyes and mouth wide, trying to absorb the abrupt shift from tranquillity to this overwhelming city chaos.

"What are those?" She exhaled, taking his hand as she walked alongside him.

5

"Cars," August replied. "You had cars in 1912, didn't you?"

"Yeah, but not like these," she marvelled. "These are so fast and small... so efficient."She gasped softly, walking past a parked car and slowly running her hand across the paintwork.

"I can't even begin to imagine what the world is like now."

"There's a lot to catch up on," August said with a grin. "But I'll show you everything."

"Thank you," Josie moved away from the road and ran to keep up with him.

"Sure. Is there anything you want to do first?"

"Yes. I'd like to try on modern clothing."

"You want to go clothes shopping? Really?"

"Unless you want me to walk around in this out of date dress then yes I do."

"I wouldn't mind, it's a nice dress."

She raised her eyebrows and cocked her head, looking up as he tousled his hair.

"Fine." He laughed, throwing his head and arms back dramatically. "Come on."

Josie's eyes widened with wonder as she stepped into the bustling shopping centre, her senses overwhelmed by the sight of modern fashion and the sound of vibrant chatter. The colourful displays and stylish mannequins in the shops caught her attention, and she found herself drawn towards the windows, her hands pressed against the glass.

"My god, you have well and truly ruined good fashion. I mean— do you not want to look smart?"

He snorted, peeling her hand away from the glass and leading her inside the shop. "It's all about comfort, Josie."

"Hm..."

"What, you don't like it?"

"Do *you* like it, I mean more than this dress?"

He looked her up and down, smiling. "Well fashion now is not as fancy as this, but at least it's practical."

"Fair enough. So, Mr know it all, what do modern girls wear on a regular day?" she asked, glancing around the store with curiosity. "I take it corsets and feathers aren't as popular?"

"No, I think they died out when people realised breathing and moving comfortably was kind of important." August quipped, smiling warmly. "But seriously, you can wear whatever makes you feel comfortable and confident. Let's pick out a few styles, and you can try them on to see what you like."

"Well thank god for modern fashion then. I like the idea of breathing."

They browsed through the racks and Josie ran her fingers over the fabrics, absorbing the textures and patterns. The music in the shop hummed quietly in the distance and she wore a faint smile as she collected an armful of assorted clothes. August pulled out a pair of blue flared jeans and handed them to her. "How about these?" he suggested, his eyes searching hers for approval. "They're hip and versatile."

"Hip?"

"Like... current fashion trends."

"Hm." She took them and held them against herself, examining the denim and the way it fell gracefully from her hands. Her reflection in the nearby mirror captured the uncertainty in her eyes, and she shook her head. "I don't know how I feel about them. They're new and—"

"Well, there's always a first time for everything," August encouraged with a warm smile. "Why don't you try them on and see how they feel? It's okay." His eyes moved between hers, and he cupped her face in his hands. Josephine nodded slowly and swallowed, her heart beating a little faster as she disappeared into the dressing room. She puffed out her cheeks and exhaled as she placed the rest of the clothes onto the bench, before slipping into the jeans. The cool fabric embraced her legs, and she marvelled at the comfort they offered. She hesitated at the entrance of the dressing room, her fingers fidgeting with the hem of the faded green t-shirt she had paired with the jeans. August's eyes lit up as she stepped towards him.

"Wow, you look fantastic!" he exclaimed, his genuine admiration evident in his voice. "The jeans fit you perfectly, and the t-shirt looks brilliant!"

A shy smile spread across her face, and a newfound confidence filled her. "It's different, but I like it," she admitted, her cheeks reddening. "I never thought trousers could be so comfortable."

Her hesitation melted away, and she picked out an emerald green dress, and her eyes widened as she watched the cotton pleats drift down the side of her legs in the mirror. "August! Come and look at this!" She giggled, parting the curtain as she twirled in front of the mirror, catching August's admiring gaze as he pulled the curtain across.

"Wow this is... this one is definitely my favourite on you," he marvelled with a boyish grin. "You look absolutely beautiful. Come on, let's pay for these, and we can go home." He stepped out and closed the curtain, leaving her beaming at her reflection in the mirror. She folded the clothes and carried them out into a neat pile, wearing a newfound apricity on her face as August paid for everything.

"Thank you, have a nice afternoon. Josie, are you ready?"

"Yes," she beamed, smoothing down the pleats in her dress. "I'm keeping this on."

"Good, you look beautiful."

"And you look like an eejit." She lightly hit his arm, and grabbed his hand, walking out of the shopping centre alongside him. "I'm joking. Thank you for taking me shopping." She leaned her head on his shoulder, gesturing at the bags. August smiled, squeezing her hand. "You don't need to thank me," he said softly. "I'm just glad I can help. Taxi!"

A yellow cab pulled up to the curb and August opened the door for her, stepping aside

"What?" She darted her eyes from his face to the inside of the car, biting her lip. "No... Au—"

"You can get in, it's okay."

"Is she okay?" The taxi driver sighed, restlessly tapping his hands on the steering wheel.

"Yeah, yeah, she's just sceptical about cars... thinks they're prone to crash or... Come on Josie, it's safe, I promise."

"Are you sure?"

He looked into her eyes and took her hand. "Positive."

She exhaled, rubbing her head. "Fine, but if anything goes wrong, I'm holding you personally accountable, eejit."

"Is that a thing with you, calling people eejits?"

"Nope. It's just for you."

"Wow, I do feel special."

As they stepped into the taxi, Josie's nervousness resurfaced, but she clung to August's hand, watching as the scenery became blurs, as the cars lined up to wait at the red light and went on the green light, she watched people going about their days, playing their roles in the play of life.

"Are you okay?"

"Yes, but what are they holding to their ears?"

"Phones."

"Telephones?"

"Kinda. But you can basically do anything on them. Photos, maths equations, calling someone. There's more information on one of those than in any book you've ever read."

"Do you have one?"

"Yes."

The taxi driver beamed, looking in the rearview mirror. "Are you a time traveller or something? How do you not know what a phone is?"

Josephine scowled at him in the mirror, choosing to ignore his comment. "Do you think I should cut my hair?"

"Why do you ask?"

"It's just... I've barely seen any girls with long hair today. I don't think I fit in."

August looked at her, his eyes warm as they traced her face. "You don't need to fit in. Your hair is beautiful just the way it is," he replied with a soft smile, curling a strand around his index finger, and releasing it into a curl. "It's a reminder of your past."

"But what if it's outdated now?"

August puffed out his cheeks, meeting her gaze with unwavering admiration. "Fashion may change over time, but true beauty is timeless. Your hair is a treasure, and it will never go out of style."

A blush crept onto her cheeks. "Thank you for being so patient and understanding. This would have been much harder without you."

August's eyes softened, and he sank lower into his seat. "I wouldn't have it any other way. We're in this together, Josie, and I'm here to support you every step of the way."

"To be honest, I couldn't see myself with short hair."

"No?"

"No." She admitted, her heart fluttering in his chest at his reassurance as the car came to a standstill. "We've arrived, sir."

"How much will it be?" August's voice tapered out as Josie turned her eyes to the building which towered above the bustling streets, touching the heavens themselves. Rows of large windows adorned its walls, offering panoramic views of the ever-changing cityscape.

The door opened and her trance was broken.

"Come on, we're home."

Chapter Three

Come, Josephine, in my Flying Machine – Ada Jones

"Do you know what a lift is?"

From the first floor, Josie's gaze was drawn to the imposing building that soared skyward, her hand covering her forehead as she squinted, taking in all of the windows.

"I've heard of them. There were a few on *Titanic*."

"Did you go in it?"

"No, I was in 3rd Class."

"Well, you don't need to be a certain class to use this one. Come on." Guiding her into the lift, he pressed the button marked "15" and the doors moved inwards, closing them in.

"Woah, this is strange. How do they work?"

"Well, the lift operates through these ropes, attached to the car we're standing in right now. They loop around a specialised pulley, a sheave, which grips the hoist ropes with grooves. When the sheave rotates, the ropes move, and we either go up or down."

She nodded, smiling slightly. "You know a lot."

"I like to learn."

"Eejit."

"Wow, the Irish in you is *really* showing. How many times have you called me an eejit just today?"

"I've got plenty more where that came from, you gobshite."

"Gobshite? That's a good one."

"You think?"

"Yes, just please never call me that. Let's stick with eejit."

With a soft chime, the lift doors opened, revealing the corridor outside. Josie stepped out, her senses adjusting to the hallway. The walls were adorned with abstract art, each piece a splash of colour. August's apartment was just a short distance away. As they walked, Josie's gaze flickered from door to door, absorbing the modern intricacies of the place – the sleek design, the LED lights, and the bright ambiance.

"You design things weirdly."

"No, you view things weirdly." Reaching his apartment's door, August pulled out a keycard and with a swipe, the door clicked open. "Make yourself at home," August offered, his voice warm as he gestured towards the living area.

August's apartment stood as a sanctuary on the fifteenth floor, a realm elevated above the bustling cityscape below. Josie's gaze landed on a guitar nestled in the corner, accompanied by a knitted blanket gracefully draped across a nearby sofa. The room exuded a gentle warmth, suffused with the faint, lingering scent of sandalwood.

"Who made the blanket?" A smile painted itself on her face from ear to ear, and her cheeks glowed with affection.

"My mom."

Josie raised her head, running her hands across the soft fabric. "She's good at knitting."

"She was the best." Her fingers paused on the fabric, and her eyes, once lost in the details of the blanket, held a hint of sadness and longing. She swallowed, her emotions catching in her throat and her smile fading into a frown.

"I'm sorry." She slowly raised her eyes to his face and he flashed a weak smile.

"Don't be. You didn't know. I've never let anyone touch it. It holds too many memories, too much pain."

Approaching the window, Josie's gaze was met by the sprawling expanse of the city below, its twinkling lights akin to stars brought down to Earth. The sight was awe-inspiring, almost dizzying. A cityscape in summer unfolded before her, a symphony of vibrant colours, bustling streets, and endless possibilities. She moved over to the guitar, noticing how its mahogany body caught the syrupy light, and she brushed her fingers against its curves.

"Do you play?"

"I used to."

"Not anymore?"

"No. It's more... decorative." He paused, looking down at his feet and then back up to her face. "So, uh, would you like something to eat? I could make some pasta for dinner. Do you like bolognese?"

"Sure."

"Alrighty. Sit down. I'll get you some water."

"Go raibh maith agat."

He blinked. "What did you say?"

"Thank you."

Outside the window, the sun gracefully dipped lower, tracking towards the horizon, painting the sky in hues of gold and crimson. It was a warm evening, the sky dappled with gold and the lush green palm trees swaying in the soft summer breeze.

"Do you ever wonder about travelling through time?" Josie asked, her eyes searching August's face for a response, as she twisted some noodles around the prongs of her fork.

"It's a nice idea, but I think it would be a challenge. You only really see this type of thing in Sci-fi movies."

"What's that?"

"Science fiction. Movies are like... moving pictures. You had those, didn't you?"

"Yes, we had movies, sort of, but nothing sci-fi... or really anything longer than 15 minutes...that's how long our reels allowed for. How long are movies now?"

"As long as you want them to be."

"Really? So you could make a movie that's, say, four hours long?"

"Yes. Kenneth Branagh's 1996 movie Hamlet."

"As in Shakespeare?"

"That's the one."

"Could you show me a movie?"

August chuckled, his features alight with amusement. "Of course. What are you in the mood for?"

"Something you love more than any movie in the world." Josie suggested.

His grin widened. "In that case, *'The Sound of Music'* it is." With a determined glint in his eyes, he stood up from the table and stretched his arms above his head. "I'll go grab the DVD and some popcorn," he declared, his voice brimming with excitement. Josie watched with curiosity as he headed towards the nearby shelf, his movements purposeful. Minutes later, he returned, clutching a DVD case. The cover was adorned with vibrant artwork which captured her attention, and her heart skipped a beat.

"It's beautiful!" She took it in her hands and turned it over, running her hands over the writing and handing it back. He smiled, taking the disc out and placing it into the dvd player. "What's it about?"

"It's about this woman called Maria who becomes a governess to seven children and teaches them all to love, be courageous and to sing. It's so beautiful, Josie. Just wait until you see it!" His grin widened as he settled back onto the couch, carefully balancing a popcorn bowl between them.

The scent of buttered popcorn wafted through the air, mingling with the anticipation that filled the room. As the screen flickered to life, Josie's eyes softened, absorbing the picturesque beauty unveiled in the opening scenes of the movie. Rolling hills, draped in the verdant embrace of lush meadows, stretched into the horizon. The alpine landscape, with its majestic peaks crowned by sunlight, painted a tranquil tableau against the azure sky. The quaint village nestled at the foothills exuded charm, its rustic architecture harmonising with the splendour surrounding it. Sunlight danced upon the meandering river, casting a golden glow that embraced the enchanting scenery. Josie raised her eyebrows, her mouth wide as she became captivated by the cinematic symphony of nature. August spread the knitted blanket over both of them, and her fingers brushed against the fabric again, and a jolt of shock coursing through her. Her lips parted with a gentle sigh, and her eyes softened.

"August—" She looked over to him, watching his shaky hands press to the crease of his eyes, drying them.

"It's okay. I want you to use it." Her breath caught, and her eyes welled up with unshed tears. In that moment, as the music rang from the speakers, she felt an overwhelming sense of safety with him. She lowered her hands which she had raised in protest and leaned into his shoulder, feeling wanted, understood, and supported in a way that went beyond any words she could have said to him. Lowering her hands, Josie leaned into him, watching as the screen faded, and the end title screen became emblazoned in yellow and orange drifted towards her. August wrapped an arm around her and beamed down at her, their eyes meeting in a sea of tears. Her lips parted into a small smile.

"Are you okay? Did you like it?"

"Was it a true story? Did the Germans invade Austria?"

"Yes, there were two world wars, this was the second."

"Did people die?"

"Yes. About 70 million." Josie's hand drifted to her face, more tears falling, her eyes flickering across his as he swallowed, moving closer to her. "But the Von Trapps fled to America. They were safe."

"You know alot about them."

"I told you, I like to learn." She bit her lip, grinning from ear to ear as she lightly hit his arm. Her cheeks were glowing like pink dahlias, brighter than spring's sunlight. He looked at her, flashing a toothy grin back, his eyes sparkling with wonder.

A girl from 1912 should not belong, should not fit into his world, but yet she did.

"Who played Maria? I won't know her, but I just... want to know."

"An actress called Julie Andrews, why?"

"She's very beautiful. Don't you think? Like almost ethereally so."

"Yes, she is."

The hours waned, and August and Josie ventured to the park, the knitted quilt trailing across Josie's shoulders as they sat down by the river. The sun was lower in the sky, but the sky was a splendid cerulean colour, dappled with gold. The river sparkled with the embers of the light and meandered behind them with a gentle ease.

"Ever heard of these, Josie?" August showed his phone screen to her. "They're called aeroplanes. This one is an A380. It's the largest and fastest passenger airliner in the world. They have four engines."

A mixture of awe and nostalgia filled Josie's eyes as she cupped the phone in her hands. "Wow. Aeroplanes... We used to dream of them in my time. We had a song about them too."

"What is it? I can put it on."

"Oh no, that's okay." She looked down into her lap, the melody coming back in a distant memory, a dream that she never thought could recur. She laughed slightly, toying with her fingers. "You won't like it."

"Aw, Josie! Come onnnn!"

"Fine! It's 'Come, Josephine in my Flying Machine."

He tapped on his phone. "Flying machine? Like those magnificent men? That's so cute, you really were dreamers."

"Don't bother putting it on. I doubt it's still known with all the fancy songs you have these days. You won't like it."

Soon the music spilled through his phone speaker and Josie looked up, her eyes wide with recognition. She hummed the tune, swaying to the beat as the sound of a phonograph crackled, dancing with memories of a time bygone.

"I used to think they wrote this song about me." She tightened the blanket around her and looked down to where her hands were plucking the grass. "I used to dream of seeing one fly above the clouds like an eagle. Novelty is always exciting. It's nice to see how they've evolved, you know that A3... whatever it was called. Is there anything you're excited for? Have they invented flying cars yet?"

He suppressed a laugh, placing his phone onto the grass, and leaning back onto his hands. "A380. And no, there are no flying cars yet."

"Are they safe?"

"Absolutely. You have a one in 5,000 chance of dying in a car accident and only a one in 7.9 million chance of dying in a plane crash."

"Well those statistics don't make me want to get into a car *ever* again. But one day, you can take me on a plane, if you like."

"I'd be honoured to."

The moon rose in the sky and the soft drone of cars became quieter as August and Josie made their way back to the apartment, up the lift, and took a sleepy glance at the city stretched out below their feet. The possibilities were endless, stretching like threads of a story waiting to be woven.

Chapter Four

Bitter Sweet Symphony — The Verve

August closed the curtains in his room, shutting out the traces of the chalky moonlight.

"You take my bed, I'll take the sofa," August whispered with a tired smile. The room exhaled a sigh of warmth as he gestured towards his bed. Josie stood with her hand on the bedpost, uncertainty flickering in her eyes, the weight of the unfamiliar present pressing upon her. Her eyes dropped, fingers fidgeting as uncertainty welled up. With a deep breath, she raised her gaze to meet his, masking the apprehension that lingered behind her glance.

"No, that's not fair. It's your bed, I'll take the sofa. I'll be fine. I—"

"Josie, it's okay, really. Anyway, it's memory foam. Another modern thing for you to try." With a gentle reassurance, August handed her a soft, worn t-shirt. "You can wear this," he said, his voice a gentle lullaby that echoed through the room, as he tucked a strand of hair behind her ears. "Go on, It's okay. I'll be next door if you need me, but I'll leave you to get changed. Goodnight, Josie."

August grabbed a pillow from his bed and smiled, leaving her alone with her thoughts. She exhaled, the weight of the day's discoveries settling around her like a cocoon. Pulling the t-shirt across her body, she found comfort in its softness, like a lifeline connecting her to the past as she ventured into the uncertain embrace of the present. She wrapped her arms around herself and looked around the room. The window was slowly ajar, allowing the gentle trickles of wind and the sound of the rushing of the traffic outside to create a serenity around her as she sat on the edge of the bed, overlooking the blinking city lights. She was a lifetime away from the world she knew but this was her second chance, and second chances must be seized. With a smile dappled on her face, she sunk into the bed and readied herself for her second lifetime of adventure. "Eejit" She whispered, closing her eyes.

The night draped itself over the city, a quilt of distant stars and soft murmurs of life outside, and Josie found herself sinking into the plush memory foam mattress, enveloped by the warmth of the duvet. Just as she began to drift into sleep, the tranquillity of the night was shattered by the sudden roar of a helicopter, piercing through the silence and jolting her awake. Josie's heart pounded in her chest as she jolted upright in bed. The covers flew from her trembling hands, scattering across the room as she landed on the floor with a resounding thud. A shiver coursed down her spine, her breaths coming in shallow gasps as she scanned the darkness, her mind racing with panicked thoughts. She pressed a hand against her chest, feeling the rapid beat of her heart, and darted her eyes around the room, noticing the orange glow of a street light flickering faintly down below and the patter of footsteps approaching the room.

"Hey, it's okay," he whispered, kneeling beside her, and draping the blanket over her shoulders. Slowly, like the fading crescendo of a symphony, her heartbeat found its rhythm once more, and she exhaled.

"Come on, let's get you off the floor." He lifted her up, and lowered her gently back into bed, sitting beside her.

"What was it?"

"A helicopter. Don't worry, it's kind of like a flying machine, just smaller and it flies a lot lower so it's a little more annoying. Are you okay though?"

"No, I am, but it reminded me of when the ship broke in half." Josie's breaths were shallow, and her eyes wide as she sunk her head back down on one of the pillows. "Sorry for waking you up."

His eyes softened. "Don't be. I was awake anyway."

"Because of me? Because you're on the sofa? You gave your blanket to me. Weren't you cold?"

"No, no of course not, Josie. The sofa's fin—"

"Come on. Share the bed with me." She urged, watching him blink in the dim light, his smile fading.

"Josie—"

"No. I'm not taking no for an answer," she asserted, her voice carrying determination. "Get your pillow and get back in here."

"Bossy."

"What?"

"Nothing," he replied, his heart racing as he left the room. "I guess the whole 'Irish people are stubborn' thing is true."

"Éist do bhéal!"

Morning soon tiptoed in, casting a golden glow through the windows. The aroma of bacon and eggs cascaded in the air, mixing with the scent of the warm breeze drifting in from outside. Josie walked out of the bedroom, the blanket still wrapped around her shoulders as she watched August move in the kitchen, dancing to the hum of the traffic and the summer breeze drifting in through the window.

"Hey, good morning! What do you want to do today?" he asked, serving two eggs onto her plate. Josie's eyes sparkled. "Can we go see the flying... aeroplanes?"

August chuckled, his eyes creasing, "sure, if you like." He sat beside her, handing her a knife and fork. "By the way, can I ask you something about last night?"

"Yeah, of course."

"I, uh..." he hesitated, rubbing the nape of his neck. "Are you comfortable with me?" Her eyes met his, an unspoken understanding passing between them. "Yes, of course. Why do you ask?"

A faint, reassuring smile tugged at his lips. "It's just... normally, you don't sleep in the same bed as someone you've only known for a day."

Josie's gaze softened as her fingers traced patterns. "Well, trust isn't about time, it's about a feeling, remember? And I feel like I've known you much longer than a day."

A flicker of gratitude danced in his eyes as he met her gaze. "No reason not to trust me, huh?" She mirrored his smile, her voice gentle. "No, of course not. Why, did it make you feel uncomfortable?"

"I don't know, maybe. A little."

She nodded pensively and looked down to her lap, a silence settling between them, and the weight of unspoken thoughts hanging in the air like the promise of a new day. The sun's warm fingers reached through the window, casting a gentle glow that seemed to paint their uncertainty with a touch of hope. August turned his gaze toward the window, his eyes tracing the patterns of sunlight dancing across the floor.

"Right, we better get going then. It takes about half an hour to get there. Have you finished with your plate?" Josie nodded, rose from her seat, and made her way to the kitchen. A contented smile lingered on her lips as she glanced back at him, a silent acknowledgment of the connection they were building.

They packed a simple picnic, a slice of comfort amid the sprawling expanse of the city, and got in the car. August slid behind the wheel, the car's engine humming to life like a quiet symphony of adventure. As the sunroof smoothly slid down, the car's interior was flooded with a torrent of sunlight, turning her vision into an expanse of glaring whiteness, leaving her momentarily disoriented. Josie moved her hands over her face and August reached into the glovebox.

"You'll need these. They're sunglasses."

"I know, we had these, you eejit." She tried them on and looked at herself in the front view mirror, nodding in approval. As the car glided down the road, Josie's face lit up with wonder, absorbing the world with bright eyes. They drifted around, the cityscape slowly being replaced by an ever-changing tableau of suburbs, open fields, and distant rolling hills. Her gaze darted from one sight to another, her lips slightly parted in awe as the scenery unfolded before her. The wind tousled her hair, carrying with it the scents of blooming flowers and freshly cut grass. It was a moment of peace in a world that moved so quickly. Each grass blade on the hillside held the quiet constancy of the last, basking in the unwavering sun. In the city, time hurried by, rushing to get through endless meaningless days, but as they drove down the winding road in an open top car, time seemed to stand still. Josie's eyes moved from the hills back to the interior of the car, her attention drawn to the radio dashboard. The array of buttons, dials, and numbers intrigued her and she hesitantly reached a hand over. A small smile tugged at her lips as she drew closer, her fingers hovering above the controls.

"What does this do?"

He glanced over, biting his lip as he tried to contain a smile. "Try it."

With a cautious touch, she pressed a button, and a burst of sound filled the car's interior. Notes of music flowed from the speakers, filling the space with lilting melodies. Her eyes lit up as the rhythm pulsed through her, a connection between her past and this new reality.

"What is it?" Josie's voice danced with curiosity.

"Bitter Sweet Symphony! A brilliant song!" August's eyes lit up as the music flowed from the speakers, filling the car with a familiar melody. "Make it louder, turn it up!"

Josie's brow furrowed in a mix of excitement and confusion. "What? How?"

August chuckled, his fingers deftly navigating the array of buttons and dials on the radio's dashboard. "Like this," he said, twisting a button with a fluid motion. The music swelled, the notes transforming into a wave that enveloped them, its energy intertwining with the air they breathed. Josie's eyes widened as if she had tapped into a hidden magic, her senses drowning in the newfound richness of sound. The notes intertwined like threads of memory, stitching together a tapestry of emotions that time had both woven and weathered.

"It's so beautiful!" Josie exclaimed, tapping her feet to the beat. "Modern music is so good!"

"Some of it is." He turned a corner, and she watched as the grass of the plane spotting garden welcomed them with a soft embrace beneath the boundless sky. She eagerly opened the car door, her steps light as she skipped toward a lush patch of grass. Blades of grass and the occasional daisy tenderly brushed against her legs. August ambled in her direction, pocketing the car key and gracing her with a warm smile, watching as a butterfly flitted past, capturing her attention, and she ran after it. He laid the blanket on the grass and she ran back towards it, throwing herself onto the floor with a soft sigh.

"Someone's comfortable."

As she turned her head, her sunglasses slid down her nose, revealing a pair of captivating green eyes, dappled with amber and specks of blue, locking onto his. The summer heat painted her cheeks with an apple rosy glow. His lips parted, captivated by the vibrant gaze that held his attention. Her eyes wandered over his face, tracing the light freckles and the wisps of blonde curls that framed his features. August smiled, parting his lips to speak. Suddenly, a distant rumble heralded its approach—an invisible giant racing through the heavens. The anticipation hung heavy in the air, a shared breath held by them. She brought her hand to her face, shielding her sunglasses. And then, like a symphony's crescendo, a plane burst into view, its metal body cutting through the canvas of blue with a grace that contrasted its massive size.

"Oh my god! It's an aeroplane! August, look! Which one is it?"

"It's a Boeing 747."

"How do you know?"

"It's got a bump on the forward part of the deck, see?" Josie's eyes widened in astonishment, her heart echoing the thunderous applause of engines that reverberated through her chest. The plane sailed overhead, wings outstretched as it embraced the atmosphere that bore it above the clouds. She bit her lip and tapped August's shoulder, her cheeks flushing. He watched her as the plane passed, a knowing smile on his lips. He saw the reflection of her wonder in her eyes—a reflection of the dreams that had taken flight within her. Her gaze tracked the plane lowering in the sky, growing smaller as it prepared to land. Her expression remained one of awe, her eyes trailing its chemtrail long after it had vanished from sight. She sat up slowly, tears in her eyes and met August's gaze. He was laughing silently, his hand on her waist as he pulled himself up.

"Your happiness is contagious," he whispered with a warm smile.

"What?" She giggled.

He chuckled softly. "I mean, seeing you so excited about aeroplanes, it's hard not to catch some of that excitement myself. It's an excitement people tend to lose in their lives." A smile faltered at the cusp of her lips, and she fiddled with her fingers.

"I've just always been fascinated by them, you know? The idea of flying, defying gravity... It's like a dream. We were only just starting to develop them in 1912 and seeing them so real is beautiful."

He nodded, captivated by the way her eyes lit up as she spoke."It's a beautiful dream to have."

She looked down, her cheeks lightly flushed. "Sorry if I sound silly."

His gaze softened. "Not at all. I love it. Curiosity and the desire to learn are great qualities to have."

"What are your top 5 planes?"

"My all time favourite is the A380," he began, settling his hands on the blanket and leaning back. "It's known for its size, carrying up to 555 people. It's the largest passenger aeroplane ever built, offering enhanced comfort and amenities. Then, the Concorde," he continued, his voice tinged with a hint of nostalgia, "was a supersonic jet that could travel at speeds twice the speed of sound, if you. It retired in 2003, but could cross the Atlantic in less than three hours.The Boeing 777, you see, has these incredibly spacious cabins. And then there's the Boeing 737, a true witness to decades of journeys. Oh, and the A340, a competitor to the Boeing 747, but it got overshadowed by the more efficient 777 and later the Airbus A350. Still one of my favourites though."

"That's amazing. You're so lucky to have them, August." She layed back down on the blanket as another plane passed overhead, her eyes glowing in admiration. The afternoon sun bathed them in its warm embrace as they savoured cake and watched planes ascend and descend like birds in flight. Josie's gaze lingered on the massive machines, her thoughts a mosaic of awe and amazement.

"How can they look so small but be so big?"

"That's the beauty of them," August mused, his eyes tracing the arcs of flight above. "Perspective turns giants into specs."

She looked over at him, casually propped up on his elbows and gazing skyward with a tranquil smile that mirrored the peace she felt within.

"August," she began, her voice carrying the weight of the emotions that had woven through their conversation. He turned his head toward her, his eyes meeting hers in a gentle connection that needed no words. "Thank you for showing me this, life is so magical now." August's smile deepened, a soft glimmer in his eyes as he leaned in closer to her.

"The magic was always there, Josie. I just helped you remember how to look."

Chapter Five

Silver Springs — Fleetwood Mac

The sun danced toward the horizon, its gentle, amber radiance enveloping the surroundings in an ethereal aura. August and Josie, their hands moving with a deliberate grace, tenderly folded the blanket, the fabric whispering secrets only they could comprehend—a relic from their day spent at the airport. Once the blanket was safely stowed away, they got into the car, and August draped the blanket over her, watching as her eyes became heavy with the warmth of the day's adventures. A gentle smile curved her lips as she burrowed into its comforting embrace, and he reached over and brushed a strand of hair away from her forehead, his touch tender like a whispered promise. The engine hummed to life at his touch, a quiet serenade that accompanied their journey and the car glided along the road, the strains of "American Pie" flowing from the speakers, enveloping them in a melody that was both timeless and fleeting. The music painted the air with a sense of calm, creating a soft cocoon. August's steady gaze held a quiet depth of connection, his eyes tracing the contours of her face whenever the road allowed. In a suspended moment, the world outside melted away, leaving only them, drifting in time and space.

The car found its way back home. August's fingers traced patterns on the steering wheel, reluctant to disturb the peace that had settled around Josie. He turned off the engine and shifted his gaze to her, a silent question hanging in the air. *Should he wake her up?* He furrowed his brow and exhaled, moving a hand to her shoulder and tapping gently.

"Josie… Josie… we're home."

She stirred, her eyes fluttering open like the petals of a delicate flower, and blinked, adjusting to the soft light, her gaze meeting August's with a drowsy smile.

"Home already?" she whispered, her voice like a lullaby.

"Home already," August confirmed, his voice a gentle caress. "Welcome back."

Josie stretched beneath the blanket. "How long was I out?"

"Only a little while," he reassured, holding out his hand. "Come on, there's something I want to show you."

A smile tugged at her lips as she took his hand. "Lead the way, eejit."

Josie slid her legs out from under the blanket and followed August up to the apartment, a sense of intrigue building with every step. The hallway lights cast a warm, welcoming glow as they got into the lift and ascended to the fifteenth floor. August led her through the door and into the cosy living room, where soft evening light filtered through the curtains, creating a serene ambiance. He gestured to the laptop, and sat in front of it, pulling a chair beside it. "I've been planning something special to show you. Sit here." August revealed, his eyes shining with excitement as he tapped the keys. "Have you heard of Spotify?"

Josie arched her eyebrow as she settled back into the chair, snickering. "Of course not, I'm not from this century, remember?"

"Right." His nose crinkled and he turned his laptop to her. "So, it's pretty simple. You can put together a bunch of songs you like and call it a playlist. Then, you can listen to it whenever you want."

"You don't use phonographs?"

"Of course not, they're not from this century, remember?" He turned to her, and as their eyes met, a shared smile blossomed between them. She leaned in closer to the laptop, her fingers gently tracing the letters on the keys.

"This is amazing," she murmured, her heart warmed by August's thoughtfulness. "How do you listen to a song?"

"Which one do you want to listen to? You can listen to anything you like."

Her eyebrows lifted in wonder, a child discovering a hidden treasure. "Anything?"

"Yup," he confirmed with a nod, his smile infectious. "Just type in the name, and voilà."

Josie leaned closer, her eyes scanning the screen. "You know what we should do?"

August's curiosity matched hers. "What?"

"We should make one of your playlist things," she said, her voice tinged with excitement. "For our next adventure."

A laugh bubbled from his lips, the sound echoing the joy that radiated from her. "Absolutely. But there's one song we can't forget."

A mischievous glint appeared in her eyes, a silent understanding passing between them. "The 'car song'?"

"Exactly," he replied with a grin. "And it's called Bitter Sweet Symphony, you eejit!"

"Who are you calling an eejit? That's my word!"

"Sorry, I promise not to steal your trademarked insults again, eejit!"

"Watch it, gobshite."

She hovered her fingers over the keys, and then hesitantly tapped the keys. Soon, the opening notes of the song filled the room, a shared chuckle blended with the music. Their eyes met in a moment of unspoken connection, a dance of emotions that needed no translation. August pulled a chair closer to his computer, and he settled onto it, watching her fingers tapping on the keys with a mixture of familiarity and curiosity.

"What should we call our playlist?"

"Timeless," Josie suggested.

August's gaze softened, the corners of his lips curving upwards as he tapped out the letters. "I like that. Music is like a thread that connects us through time. What other songs do you want on there?" The playlist began to take shape, a digital canvas painted with notes and melodies that held stories within their folds. Josie's fingers danced over the keyboard, each key pressed a step further into the musical realm.

"So, where did you grow up?"

Josie exhaled, the soft sound carrying with it a lifetime of memories. "I grew up in Belfast, with my parents Róisín and Michael. My mother's a writer, and my father is a shipbuilder."

"Róisín? How on earth do you spell that?"

"R - O - I - S - I - N. It means little rose."

"That's nice. If Róisín is anything to go by, your middle name must be fun to spell."

"It's—"

"No Let me guess... A - E - V - A."

"Nope. Not even close. E- A- B- H- A. For someone who likes to learn, you don't know alot about Irish phonetics."

"It's never really crossed my radar."

"Your what?"

"Radar. Oh. They use radio waves to figure out how far away, at what angle, and how fast objects are moving in relation to a specific location. It's used to identify and monitor aircraft, ships, spacecraft, missiles, vehicles, as well as to map weather patterns and terrain. Anyway," August leaned in, "What was your childhood like?"

"You're such a geek!" Josie's eyes lit up as she began to paint a vivid tapestry with her words.

"I spent most of my time at the shipyard with my father. I used to sketch the gantries, the slipways, the ships... It was my way of capturing the world around me."

A sense of wonder lingered in the air as August listened, his gaze focused solely on her. Her smile was tinged with nostalgia, a delicate brush stroke on the canvas of her memories. "And then... for my 18th birthday. I boarded the *Titanic*."

He raised an intrigued eyebrow, leaning slightly closer, his chin resting on his hand. Her nod was accompanied by a soft chuckle. "Yes. Quite the birthday gift, wouldn't you say? Okay, Mr Quinn, how about you?"

"Well I, uh, grew up in a small town in Los Angeles," he began, his voice carrying a touch of nostalgia. "My parents, Iris and James, were both teachers. And Olivia, my younger sister. I was always curious, exploring the woods and fields near our house. Liv and I were partners in crime, always up to some adventure."

A playful curiosity tugged at Josie. "What about Liv?"

"What about her?"

"You talked about her in the past tense."

"Oh, right. well... she's eighteen, four years younger than me. We're quite the team, even if we did drive our parents crazy at times. We aren't as close as we used to be. Our mom— nevermind"

"What about her?"

"I-I'll tell you another time." He exhaled, blinking to push some tears back.

"Well, I'd love to meet Liv. Ooh! Can I? Today?" She clapped her hands and blinked at him, her eyes twinkling with anticipation.

"Sure, if you like. I'm sure she's free." August laughed, his warm chuckle resonating through the air like a comforting melody. He couldn't help but admire Josie's genuine excitement, which added a new layer of vibrancy to their conversation.

The night wore on, and as the stars emerged in the velvety sky, their connection remained steadfast. The laptop cast a warm glow, illuminating their faces as they shared laughter, memories, and dreams. Eventually, the notion of meeting Liv emerged, a bridge between the digital world and reality. August's fingers danced across the keys as he started a call.

"Hey, Liv, there's someone I want you to meet. This is Josephine. Can you come over?"

A face appeared on the screen, Liv's eyes wide with anticipation. "Oh, is this the infamous time traveller you incessantly text me about?"

Josie chuckled, her eyes sparkling. "Not so much of a time traveller, but—." She looked at August. "By the way, how does this work?" She leaned in closer to the screen, squinting slightly. "Is it like a video telephone?"

"Sort of. It's a video call, but with extra features. We can see and talk to each other in real-time, plus share screens and chat."

"So she's actually talking right now?"

"Well, yes."

Liv grinned, intrigued. "Well, spill the details, August. How did you two meet?"

August leaned back in his chair, a playful glint in his eyes. "It's a long story, Liv. Why don't you come over? I'll make dinner, and you can hear it firsthand."

A knowing smile crossed Liv's face. "Alright, you've got me curious. I'll be there. Give me ten minutes, you know what the traffic is like at this time."

The call disconnected and Josie looked at August, her mouth splashed with a sunny smile. He let out a soft chuckle and wrapped an arm around her. With the arrangements made, they said their goodbyes and ended the call. The room shimmered with excitement, the anticipation of the evening ahead weaving a new thread into their shared narrative. The atmosphere in August's home hummed with an undercurrent of anticipation. The table was set with care, each plate a canvas awaiting the vibrant palette of conversation. August glanced at Josie, his heart dancing to a rhythm only they could hear. Soon, the doorbell chimed, the sound echoing through the apartment like a melodious announcement. August moved towards the door, his steps light with eagerness. He swung the door open to reveal Liv, her eyes alight with curiosity.

"Hey, Liv. Come on in," August greeted, a grin spreading across his face. "Nice to see you again, how's that uni course going?"

"I've not started it yet! I've got this project to do before I start as a kind of... induction. You need to stop moving things around! Oh my... is that Josephine?"

"One thing I *didn't* tell you about Liv, Josie, is that she cannot, for the life of her, stick to one conversation."

"I have ADHD, that's not fair." Liv frowned, looking over at the girl in the green dress, watching as she rose from her seat, a warm smile on her lips, and held out her hand.

"Hi, Liv. It's nice to meet you. What's ADHD?"

"It's a neurodevelopmental disorder. Attention deficit hyperactivity disorder. It's nothing to be scared of, it just makes her interesting, doesn't it Olivia?" August explained, patting Liv's shoulder. Liv's eyes widened as she took in Josie's appearance, her expression a mix of awe and amazement.

"Wow, it's really you. August wasn't kidding. He's always been a kidder, you know, when we were younger he told me that broccoli would turn my hair green. I avoided it for weeks!" She sank down onto a chair. "What's for dinner tonight Gus?"

"It'll be broccoli if you call me that again."

"You called me Olivia first!"

Josie laughed, a melodic sound that seemed to fill the room. "He's made egg fried rice."

Dinner unfolded like a symphony of flavours and stories, the laughter and exchanged stories filling the air like a melody. Plates were passed, glasses were raised, and the conversation flowed like a river, meandering through tales of the past and dreams of the future. Liv's eyes gleamed with curiosity as she pressed a glass to her lips.

"So, Josie, what was it like on the *Titanic*? Did you actually die?"

"Liv! You can't ask her that!"

"No, no it's okay." Josie's gaze softened, her hand patting August's shoulder as a weak smile trembled on the cusp of her lips. "It was... well, something I'll never forget. The grandeur, the anticipation—it was like stepping into another world. I was only eighteen and I just... you know, Ireland to America is a pretty big change. And then, of course, the unimaginable happened."

Liv's eyebrows lowered into a frown, and she bit her lip, a deep understanding passing between them. "It must have been both beautiful and tragic."

"Exactly," Josie agreed, her eyes reflecting the weight of her memories. "But it's a part of my journey, a chapter that shaped who I am. I don't know how I died. I don't know how I got here."

"I bet the great mind of Mr August Quinn the physics teacher will be able to offer you an explanation!" Liv chuckled. "Go on."

Four expectant eyes turned to August whose eyes were narrow. He softened them and swallowed. "Well... there is the possibility that you were cryogenically frozen in time. That is, if you're into all that science fiction jazz."

"We could always take you to get tests done or—" Liv suggested.

"No. Life is meant for us to live, not to be tested on."

After dinner, they cleared the plates and were sitting in the living room, the glow of soft lamplight casting a warm ambiance.

"And that's how we ended up here," August concluded, his eyes meeting Liv's with a mixture of sincerity and hope. Liv leaned back on the couch, a contemplative expression on her face. "You know, it's pretty incredible. You two have this... connection that goes beyond everything we know. But how did you end up in the creek?"

August exchanged a glance with Josie, his heart swelling with a quiet appreciation for the bond they shared. "I don't know, but Josie has brought a unique perspective into my life. It's like... we downplay things that are actually really cool just because we're so used to them, like aeroplanes, but they're new to Josie, and exciting. It's refreshing."

Josie nodded, her gaze unwavering. "And August has given me a glimpse of a world I never thought I'd experience again."

"Talking about that, did you know they made a movie about the *Titanic*? You want to see?"

August's eyes shot up and his head shook violently as he placed a hand on Josie's shoulder, watching her breath hitch.

"Liv, no," he whispered. "Don't you think it'd be insensitive? You know, with Josie's past being in the *Titanic's* history. Don't you think the prospect of watching a movie clip could—"

Josie, her spirit undimmed by the weight of her memories, nodded contemplatively. "Stop worrying. Sure, I'd love to see it." She said, her eyes shimmering. August held his breath as Liv set her phone to the sinking scene. As the scene began to play, Josie's face displayed a cascade of emotions. Her eyes widened at the grandeur of the ship on the screen, a stark contrast to the memories she held. Grief dimmed the blueness of her eyes as she watched contemplatively on.

"They've taken quite a few liberties with the details," Josie remarked, her voice carrying a note of gentle correction. "I remember it differently, you see. It was a lot darker than this, a lot louder ... It's all a bit embellished."

August smiled at her, his nose wrinkling. "Are you okay though?"

"Yeah, of course." Josie stifled a yawn, her eyelids heavy with the weight of the day's events. "It's just a movie clip."

"But you lived through it," August reminded her.

"Honestly, I'm fine. I'm glad to have seen it. To see it from a perspective other than mine. I must admit, all this excitement has caught up with me."

August stood up, a gesture that seemed both familiar and protective. "Well then, I think it's time for you to rest. Come on."

"No! You're having your bed tonight, it's not fair."

"Wait... is there something going on between you two? You're sleeping in his bed?"

"No, nothing is going on. I'm just kind, unlike you. I'm going to take her to bed. Feel free to crash on the chair."

"That's okay, I better be going home. Nice to meet you, Josie, hopefully see you again soon."

"How about tomorrow?"

"Yes." Liv looked at August who nodded and flashed a weary smile. "Tomorrow it is. I'll be here at ten."

As the night embraced them, Josie found herself lying in his bed, the moonlight filtering through the curtains like a gentle lullaby. Her mind drifted back to the day's adventures, to the stories shared and the connections forged. The world was vast and intricate, a tapestry of moments woven together by shared laughter and understanding. She smiled. The future held wonders for her, for August. For the bond which defied the boundaries of time.

And as the night whispered its secrets to the stars, Josie drifted into dreams, a sense of belonging cradling her like the soft embrace of the blanket they had packed away earlier.

Chapter Six

Nights in White Satin – The Moody Blues
Saturday, 24th June 2023

In the relentless grip of a scorching summer sun, Josie, August and Liv found themselves drawn together, their lives converging with a languid grace that mirrored the hot summer day. Liv arrived at the door with a grin as radiant as the sun, her eyes aglow with the promise of nostalgia.

"Where are we going today?" Josie's voice, a gentle zephyr, whispered like a secret against the oppressive heat.

Liv beamed, throwing herself onto the sofa, fanning herself with her phone. "What about the dock gates, they're fun."

August's eyes narrowed as he stirred the icecubes in his glass. "I don't think exposing Josie to more ships is a good idea. You know her history."

"I know," Liv's resolve remained unyielding, her gaze fixed on a distant horizon that beckoned with forgotten memories. "But you told me that Josie used to sketch ships, didn't she? It could be therapeutic for her. And she was fine watching the clip yesterday."

"I'd love to see the ships again. But I don't have any of my equipment."

August, swayed by Josie's relentless enthusiasm, offered a reassuring pat on Josie's shoulder. "Don't worry about it, Josie. I've got more than enough. Are you sure you want to go to the docks? It won't bring up any bad memories for you, will it?"

Josie darted her eyes between his, smiling softly. "I'll be fine. I grew up by the docks. It's a part of me."

The sun scorched streets blurred into a dreamscape as their car trundled down the road, the strains of their playlist floating through the car. The terminal stood like ancient monoliths, guarding the threshold to a realm of maritime wonders. The sky, stretched wide and boundless, was painted with bold strokes of cerulean, streaked with the wisps of ethereal clouds. The sun cast a molten golden hue upon the water, transforming the ships into glistening relics of a bygone era. A car door slammed, sunglasses were put on and a sigh was expelled from Liv's lips.

"I checked Vesselfinder. There should be a cruise ship in port today."

August nodded, folding his arms. "Come on, if we walk around here, we can get a better vantage point." With a shared smile, they took off running, hand in hand, laughter carried away by the gentle caress of the sea's salty breeze. The air sparkled with a touch of enchantment as their surroundings embraced the magic of the moment. As they raced along the shore, a majestic ship emerged on the horizon, its hull a radiant white that seemed to defy the ordinary world. The scene etched itself into their hearts, destined to become a cherished memory, a fleeting yet magical moment frozen in time.

"What is she called?"

"Emerald Princess."

"She's gorgeous."

Josie tiptoed as close as the grass would allow, and sat down, a faint gasp escaping her lips. August and Liv lingered behind, taking in the ship. A flood of emotions surged as she beheld the vessel, something which had once defined her world, a world that had slipped through the hourglass of time. It had been 111 years since she last stood at the docks, 5000 miles away, her heart yearning for the embrace of the open sea. A small gasp came from her parted lips as a horn bellowed across the bay, and a faint smile drifted across her face.

"Can I sketch it?"

Nostalgia gripped her heart as August placed a pad of paper and a pencil before her. She adjusted herself on the grass, her hands trembling with a mix of longing and anticipation. Her eyes flickered up to the ships and down across her paper. She grasped the pencil in her hand and set the lead on the paper, making a soft line. Then another. Soon, a ship emerged on the page, and her eyes glowed with recognition. She traced her fingers along the paper hull, following the bridge wings and the thousands of windows leading to thousands of cabins. With each pencil stroke, she poured her feelings onto the paper, trying to capture the essence of another maritime marvel.

"This is so surreal, I've missed this so much. The last time I did this, I was drawing *Titanic*."

"It's so beautiful, Josie. You're so talented."

"Thank you. I can't believe how much ships have changed since *Titanic*."

"Well yes, they kind of had to. Now we have a thing called SOLAS, Safety of Life at Sea convention, to introduce standards for ship construction, safety equipment, and procedures. Watertight compartments, sufficient lifeboats, and improved communication and navigation technologies became standard. Oh and now, lifeboat drills are mandatory. And the bridge wings are longer now to make them easier to navigate."

Liv punched his arm. "Smartarse."

Josie smiled. "Eejit."

"Wow, I tell you groundbreaking information and I get called names. How typical."

Later in the evening, as the sun descended, the world around them transformed into a symphony of colours, a slow and hypnotic dance of light and shadow. Fiery oranges dissolved into soft pinks, and the sky deepened into twilight, casting a warm, nostalgic glow upon the scene. The ship had left, and a solitary cargo ship glided gracefully across the tranquil waters. Its polished hull glistened in the fading light, catching the last whispers of a dying breeze. Josie's face lit up with a mix of awe and nostalgia as she watched the ship, her eyes tracing the vessel's elegant silhouette against the setting sun.

"Excuse me, are you Josephine?"

Startled, Josie turned to face a stranger, placing the pencil on the paper and moving her eyes away from the docks. Their presence was an enigma against the backdrop of the setting sun. Her voice, filled with a mixture of curiosity and longing, replied, "Yes."

"Are you actually from 1912, because that is so cool, can I take a photo with you?"

Josie nodded, moving to his side, and smiling. August interjected with furrowed brows, his concern etched upon his face. The lines on his forehead deepened like the etchings on a weathered map.

"Josie, wait." He pushed the phone down and looked her in the eye. "Why is he delving into your life? Who is he?"

"I'm—-"

"Shut up!"

Josie blinked, staggering towards August, placing a hand on his cheek. "It's alright, he's just curious. I can handle it."

August closed his eyes, pinching his nose with his thumb and index finger. "Curious or not, I don't like strangers prying into your life. It's not safe, Josie. What if they wanted to run tests on you?"

"I don't want to hurt her."

"Put your goddamn phone away, and get away from her!"

Josie's frustration found its voice. Her eyes, once as serene as the tranquil sea, now held a turbulent depth, a reflection of a desire long suppressed. She moved out of the camera shot, holding up her index finger to August.

"Why are you trying to shield me from everything? I can't keep living in secrecy forever! He doesn't want to test me, he wants to take a photograph, what's so wrong with that?!"

Her eyes flicked between him, the terminal and a thin stretch of pavement. She turned away, her anger flaring even hotter as she ran onto the pavement. With her words scattered like fallen embers, Josie's heart became heavy with betrayal. Cars honked as she crossed the intersection, but she barely saw or heard them as she dragged her drawing and her soul along the roads. August called after her, his voice choked with remorse, and the world around him seemed to fade into insignificance.

"Josie! Please come back! I'm sorry!" August implored, watching after her as she disappeared. He grabbed the man by his collar and dragged him to Liv.

"Put me down!"

"Not until I have answers. How the hell do you know Josie?"

"H-he might have seen my post," Liv admitted, her voice trembling with guilt and regret. Her gaze fell to the ground, and she clenched her hands in silent anguish. August's eyes darkened, a whirlwind of anger and disappointment brewing within. His gaze bore into her face, as if searching for answers hidden deep within her. "Your post?"

Liv nodded, her voice quivering. Her gaze held the weight of regret. "I posted a picture of Josie yesterday." She sniffed, tucking her billowing hair behind her ears.

"Saying. What." He gritted his teeth.

"Saying... I don't know, that I was happy to meet a girl from 1912, that it was cool, and saying we were going to show her the cruise terminal."

"You—" August's frustration surged forth, his emotions raw in the fading light. His voice, like distant thunder, held the intensity of a storm on the horizon. His eyes narrowed and his breathing became ragged.

"I'm sorry."

"You're sorry? You've been reckless, Olivia. You posted our location for anyone to find her! You better hope Josie is safe. Take it down. Now."

August left in pursuit of Josie, his footsteps echoing the urgency of his emotions. The sun had set, and the world around them was cloaked in shadows. His breaths grew sparser, each step purposeful as he left Liv standing alone at the terminal. His mind raced, and the beauty of the surroundings went unnoticed. The evening unfurled its velvety wings, and the stars emerged, each one a beacon of hope in the vast expanse of the night sky. It was a night of shadows and secrets, where destiny wove its intricate web around them.

August ran down streets and through throngs of people searching for Josie, but she remained elusive, lost to the night. The weight of guilt and nostalgia hung heavy in the air as he slowed his footsteps and sat by the side of the fountain, placing his hands on his knees, watching the lampposts quiver with fear. His hair billowed in front of his face as he looked back. It would be easier to drive around to find her, he thought, turning back towards Liv, his phone in hand, toying with the idea to call her.

"Damn it, Josephine."

Meanwhile, Liv, standing alone beneath the celestial tapestry, gazed up at the stars, each one a reminder of their interconnectedness. Guilt gnawed at her like a relentless tide, threatening to pull her into the depths of remorse. The man had left, and she had taken sanctuary on the cool grass, her head in her hands. The faint clash of footsteps drew her attention, and she looked up to see August approaching, his steps purposeful. His anger had ebbed, replaced by a flicker of understanding. He beckoned for her to come over and she sauntered to his side.

"I was wrong to be angry with you, Liv. I'm so sorry," August admitted, leading her towards the car, opening his door and sitting inside, a lump in his throat.

"How do you know that guy anyway?"

"I don't know... he must go to my uni or something."

"Well you better find out who he is and tell him he better destroy any photos he got of her."

"I will. I'm sorry."

He smiled and started the engine.as he steered the car down the winding road, his grip on the wheel tense as Liv reached her hand to the radio.

"No, don't put the radio on. Music reminds me of her."

"Sorry. You had every right to be upset. I'm sorry for posting about her," Liv replied, her gaze fixed on the passing trees and her fingers idly tracing the edge of her mother's blanket, which was folded on the floor. As they drove in silence, the familiar scent of the blanket enveloped the car, a reminder of the loving memories they had shared with their mother. The car moved down the boulevard, and Liv moved the blanket from under her seat to on her knee.

"She uses this blanket doesn't she?"

"Josie?"

"Yes."

"Yes."

"Why?"

August briefly glanced at the blanket, his eyes glistening with emotion. "It brings her comfort, you know? In a world that's still unfamiliar to her."

"But it's yours."

"I know it's mine. But Josie is part of my life, it's my job to look after her and if she finds comfort in the blanket, I'm not going to stop her from using it. It's always brought me comfort. I know you don't like people talking about mom or using things she made but it's inevitable, and honestly talking about it really helps."

"Is that why you've told Josie what happened to her?"

He bit his lip. "I will. In my own time. She's got enough on her plate already."

Silence settled over them as the car crackled across the tarmac, orange lights spilling in through the windows as they sped past. They had been driving for what felt like an eternity, their hearts heavy with worry for Josie. The radio remained off, and the drone of cars enveloped them as they scanned the streets.

"She can't have gone far, she doesn't know her way around LA. I can't believe I let her out of my sight, we should get her a phone so we can call her or something. God! How could I be so stupid? I'm so pissed off at my—"

Liv gasped. "August! Turn down this street."

"Why?"

"Just do it for god's sake!"

August turned the steering wheel, watching a girl with copper hair and an old faded band shirt standing on the street corner, her face streaked with tears. Liv leaned out of the car window, waving her arms as August swerved to park the car.

"Josie! Stop! Please!" The urgency in her voice echoed through the quiet street, and August swiftly brought the car to a screeching halt. Without a second thought, they both jumped out and ran toward her. Josie fell to the floor, defeated. Her teary eyes locked onto his and August threw himself beside her, wrapping his arms around her shoulders

"August... Liv.... I-I'm sorry. I didn't know where to go."

He gripped her shoulders tightly, tears welling up in his eyes. "I was so worried about you, Josephine, I'm so so sorry."

His heart thudded in his chest, and his body succumbed to the exhaustion of his relief, and a rush of warmth surged through him. Unable to resist the overwhelming feeling in that instant, he leaned in and placed a kiss on her lips, gasping as he pulled away, his eyes flickering to each of hers. Her cheeks flushed with a rosy hue, and their eyes widened in mutual surprise, and time seemed to stand still. In that fraction of a second, a whirlwind of emotions spun around them - curiosity, vulnerability, and an unspoken connection. Liv watched them, her jaw slackened.

"I didn't mean to shield you, you just have to be careful now with photographs. I didn't want anything bad to happen. I care about you, Josephine. How can you be so nonchalant?"

"It used to be much easier to be nonchalant about my life. I expect now it's much more difficult." Josie's question hung in the air like a heavy fog, settling in their hearts as they grappled with the profound changes that had brought them to this moment.

She looked down, sniffling. "I'm sorry."

"No, you didn't know. The thing is now, we have a thing called social media. It's like a thing you can interact on, kind of like video calls but you can also share photographs with millions of people."

"Millions?"

"Billions even. That's why you have to be— *promise* me you'll be careful, Josephine."

"I'll be careful."

August smiled, wiping her tears and leading her to the car. Liv stepped closer, holding out their mother's blanket with trembling hands, and wordlessly wrapped it around Josie, her eyes filled with understanding and compassion. Josie accepted it with a fragile smile, feeling the comfort of their shared history and the unbreakable bond that had brought them back together. Josie gingerly sat in the front seat, her head on the head rest.

"Don't turn on the radio," Liv advised. "August didn't want to listen to music."

"No, it's okay. Music sounds great."

Josie pressed a button and music flooded the car.

"Wooh! They're playing all the good songs for you, Josie!" Liv exclaimed.

"What is it called?"

"Nights in white satin!" August revealed, tapping along to the beat. The melody of the song filled the air, its notes weaving a spell around them. With a tired smile, Josie sank into her seat, cocooned in a blanket that whispered warmth and comfort. The lyrics, like a gentle caress, flowed between her ears, creating a harmonious symphony with the night.

***

In the dimly lit living room, August and Liv found themselves curled on the sofa, engrossed in a late night gossip session. The soft glow of a single lamp illuminated their faces, casting shadows that danced along with the emotions in the room. Josie, worn out from the day, lay tucked in bed, unaware of the conversation unfolding in the quiet corners of their home.

"You love her," Liv's words cut through the stillness, her gaze fixed on August with a mix of understanding and insistence.

"I don't know," August looked over to the clock. *22:15.* The numbers glowed green in the darkness and were—

"August!"

"Hm?"

"You let her sleep in your bed, wear your clothes, and have Mom's blanket. *Oh,* and, let's not forget, you kissed her today! August, you kissed her!"

The room held its breath as August grappled with the realisation of his own actions. "I-I was worried about her," he offered, his defence echoing in the muted air.

"*No*, you *love* her," Liv declared, her conviction echoing in the room. "Don't deny it, August."

A silence settled between them, heavy with unspoken truths and the palpable tension of emotions laid bare. August sighed, a conflicted soul caught between the burgeoning feelings he dared not name and the fear of what acknowledging them might entail. He bit his lip and looked around the room, to the green glow of the clock. *22:17.*

"It's too soon to do anything about it." He whispered, raising his eyebrows. "Don't tell her, Liv,"

"I won't tell her. *You* need to," Liv asserted, her eyes holding August's gaze, an unspoken understanding lingering in the room like a silent melody. She stood up, patting his arm. "I'm going home. Goodnight. Don't have too much fun with your girlfriend."

Chapter Seven

Only Time – Enya

Josie sat across from August in the living room, a tapestry of twilight's gentle glow weaving a warm, ethereal light through the windows. The soft radiance painted a soothing canvas around them, and the smile he bestowed upon her had over the course of two weeks delicately woven its way into the fabric of her heart. With a gentle grace, she moved to sit beside him, their limbs naturally intertwining in an embrace that transcended words, and he closed his eyes, leaning into her hair.

"August?"

"Mhm?"

"You're a physics teacher, aren't you?"

"Yes," he replied, rubbing her arm. "Why?"

A hopeful smile played on her lips as she continued, "Could I teach art at your school?" He studied her with a tender admiration, his eyes conveying a mix of awe and encouragement, as if he had known her for a lifetime.

"If that's what you want to do," he whispered, his voice a soft serenade of devotion.

"Do you think I'll be good at it?"

"Well, you've achieved so much in such a short time," he reached for her hand, fingers gently intertwining with hers. "I think you can do anything you want. Do you?" With a soft, genuine smile, he traced the lines of her face with his eyes, lingering on each detail as if committing them to memory.

"I do," Josie whispered, her lips parting with a gasp as her eyes locked onto his. Their shared smile felt like a promise, a bridge between two souls yearning for connection. Her cheeks bloomed into dahlias as she looked down. She was finally becoming a part of the modern world, a world where dreams could be realised. *Lived.*

August leaned forward, his fingers dancing gracefully across the sleek surface of an iPad resting on the coffee table. "Here, let me introduce you to something incredible," he said, his voice infused with a warm enthusiasm.

"What is it?"

"It's an iPad," he replied, a fond smile gracing his lips. "And it's a canvas for your art. Look here, this is the pen, a stylus. You can choose different colours by tapping here, and to draw, simply touch the screen like this," he explained, his words a soothing current. "It's your digital palette, Josie, and the possibilities are endless. Go on, have a go." He handed her the iPad and the stylus, and she took it in her shaking hands, drawing a squiggle on the screen.

"Ah! How do I rub it out?"

"Undo. Just here."

Her lips curved into a smile as she sat up, turning to face him, the screen away from his eyes. "Now, don't move!" She moved the pen across the screen, drawing lines and darting her eyes to look back up at him every now and then. "I'm going to draw you!"

Each stroke of the stylus unfurled a chapter in their shared destiny, an artist's masterful touch sculpting a canvas of emotions and love. Her gaze flitted between his features and the artwork emerging beneath her touch. In the midst of the moment, his laughter rang out like a lyrical melody, a warm and affectionate symphony filling the room, and she shot him a playful glare, her eyes dancing with mirth.

"Hey, I'm trying to capture your essence here. Don't make me mess up," she protested.

"Yes, but my essence is laughter and warmth. "This." He dragged his finger around the shape of his face. Is my essence."

"Right. Sorry."

Time yielded to the eternal, and the world outside dissolved, leaving only two souls intertwined, glowing with a divine light. She poised the stylus again and drew two almond shapes, filling them in with cyan.

"You have lovely drawable eyes."

August's smile deepened. "You have a gift, Josie," he said, his eyes never leaving hers. "Artistry flows through your veins. Now hurry up so I can see!"

"Okay! Here!" She turned the screen around to him and watched his eyes glimmer as he reached for the iPad. His eyes illuminated with a quiet wonder, and for a fleeting moment, the world fell away. His hand drifted to his lips, in silent awe as his eyebrows darted up.

"You never fail to impress me, Miss Melrose," he exhaled. The air held its breath for a moment as their gazes lingered, each silently expressing the depth of their connection. He smiled at her, noticing her smile falter.

"Hey, what's wrong? You did a great job. I love it." He asked, placing the iPad onto the table. Josie took a deep breath, her eyes glistening with unshed tears as they flickered across his face. "Is it normal to feel like you don't belong in this world, like you're always doing something wrong?"

"Hey, why do you say that?" He took her hand, rubbing the pad of his thumb over her knuckles as she flicked her eyes from his face to her lap.

"This— everything is so new to me, and I just feel like I should have died in 1912. I mean— why am I the only person from *Titanic* who came back? Do you ever get that?"

His eyes softened as he reached out and gently touched her hand. "That's survivor's guilt talking, Josie. I think most of us have moments where we question our place in this world. I can't say I've experienced exactly what you have, but I do understand the feeling of not quite fitting in. Sometimes, it's as if life has given us a second chance, and we're left wondering why. But you know, maybe there's something unique that you're meant to contribute to this world, something that only *you* can offer. You becoming an art teacher will be your beautiful contribution. Plus you're adding so much to my life."

Josie's breath quivered, her teary eyes locking onto August's. She swallowed hard, her heart racing, feeling his words touching something deep within her. In that moment, as their hands met, she felt a profound connection, a reassurance that her second chance was meant for something truly meaningful.

"You always know the right things to say, August. What else do you know?" August's gaze intensified. "I know you. You're the most beautiful, kind, and talented person I've ever met." Her lips parted as a tear traced a glistening path down her cheek.

"Is that why you kissed me?" She whispered. August looked down, his expression a mix of longing and regret. "I kissed you because I couldn't bear the thought of you leaving. I was scared of losing what we have, losing you." He brought her in for a hug, his fingers tracing patterns along her back, as if he could hold her together with the sheer strength of his touch.

"You belong here, Josie. I'm so happy we met."

Chapter Eight

The Parting Glass – Celtic Woman

"I called Lea," August announced, his voice gentle, as walked into the living room and handed her a mug of tea. The steam curled upwards, carrying with it a comforting aroma.

"Who?" Josie frowned, her gaze fixed on the swirling patterns in her tea.

"Lea Cameron. The headmistress at my school," August explained, taking a seat next to her.

"Oh?"

"She said she wants to meet you." Seconds ticked by, a contemplative silence hanging in the air. "When?"

"Today, midday," August replied, his tone filled with a touch of anticipation. "What do you think?"

She gently placed her tea aside, and then drew August into her arms. In the tenderness of their connection, August could sense the myriad emotions coursing through her – the blend of curiosity, nerves, but, above all, a profound appreciation for the deep and timeless bond they had built together.

"Thank you."

***

"So, Josie, August said you were interested in teaching here at Fairside," Lea asked, her voice a melodious blend of curiosity and anticipation. She leaned forward in her spacious office, the midday sunlight streaming through the office's grand window, casting a warm, golden glow across the room. Josie, seated across from her, felt her heart pound in her chest. The office exuded an air of erudition, its walls adorned with floor-to-ceiling bookshelves, filled with books that had weathered the passage of time.

"Yes, Ma'am," Josie replied, squeezing August's hand. The room had an intoxicating scent of aged paper and the soft hum of the antique clock in the corner.

"Great! I just need to get some details from you if that's okay?" Lea had her pen poised above a blank notepad, and raised an eyebrow. Josie nodded, her eyes flitting across the room, taking in the shelf upon shelf of books.

"Of course."

"Great! When is your date and place of birth... just for your file?" Lea asked, her eyes focused intently. Josie hesitated, her gaze momentarily fixed on a photograph placed on the desk. The picture showed a younger Lea, surrounded by a group of children, a snapshot of her dedication to education. It emitted an air of nurturing authority, setting Josie at ease.

"I, uh, I'm from Belfast, um...."

August leaned in closer, his voice a gentle breeze in her ear. "You can tell her, she knows you're a time traveller." Josie met August's understanding gaze, her uncertainty dissipating, replaced by a hint of shared humour.

"I am not!" she whispered back with a wry smile. "Um, my date of birth is the 15th July 1894."

Lea's pen moved gracefully, etching these details onto the page. "Making you... 129, correct?"

Josie nodded, a twinkle of pride in her eyes. "Correct."

"But actually... eighteen?" Lea inquired with a raised eyebrow, a trace of curiosity in her voice.

"Yes, ma'am."

Lea leaned back, a contemplative look on her face. "Hm. It's an unusual circumstance, that's for sure. But Mr. Quinn has shown me the drawings you did at the cruise terminal, and he assures me that you're very passionate about what you do. I would love to offer you the position, if you want?"

Josie's eyes darted to August, a mix of enthusiasm and a touch of hesitance playing in her gaze. Their eyes locked, and he responded with a reassuring squeeze of her hand. With a bright smile, she nodded. "I can't wait. Thank you so much, ma'am."

Lea smiled warmly, "Please, call me Lea. I'll send you the details. May I take your email address down, please?"

Josie blinked, momentarily bewildered by the unfamiliar term. "My what?"

"Email address." August explained. "It's like mail, but on your phone or laptop. Can you send me the details for now, Lea, and I'll make Josie an email address? It seems we may need to enrol you onto a crash course on modern communications, hey."

A soft chuckle escaped Josie's lips. "Sure."

"Well, thank you for bringing her, August. And see you both soon for the first week of the semester! Nice to meet you, Josie."

As they walked out of Lea's office, Josie's steps felt lighter, and her heart swelled with a sense of awe. The gleaming linoleum floors, and the soft hum of computers, were all part of this new world that unfurled before her. Her gaze drifted to August, his smile a beacon of reassurance, a lighthouse guiding her through uncharted waters as they traversed the halls.

Then, like a burst of sunlight through a cloudy sky, Josie couldn't contain her excitement as she exclaimed "I did it!"

August's face lit up, his eyes warm with pride. "Yes, you did! I'm so happy for you."

Their eyes locked, words unnecessary as they allowed time to unfold. Josie, her eyes sparkling with a sense of adventure, broke the silence. "So, what's on the agenda for the rest of the afternoon then?"

"I say we revel in your victory. Let's go get lunch."

"Hm... sophisticated language and food, you really know your way to a girl's heart."

"I do my best to keep things interesting. Josephine."

***

The restaurant they chose had a cosy, inviting atmosphere, with dimmed lights and soft jazz music creating a warm, intimate ambiance. They found a tucked-away table, the soft glow of a flickering candle casting a loving hue over their evening.

"You know, Josie, they say the way to a woman's heart is through their stomach."

Josie laughed, her eyes sparkling. "*Oh*, is that why you brought me here? To steal my heart with food?"

August grinned, sipping from his glass. "Well, they also say knowledge is the key to the heart. How about this, I'll teach you something new over dinner?

Then I can steal your heart in more ways than one." Josie's eyes widened, a spark of intrigue dancing within them. Her playful smile hinted at the thrill of a new adventure as she leaned in, urging him to share. "Go on, Professor August. Enlighten me."

August's eyes lit up with enthusiasm as he began to explain. "Alright, so, did you know that the Eiffel Tower can be 15 cm taller during the summer than in the winter?"

Josie's brows furrowed in curiosity. "Really? How's that possible?"

August chuckled, "It's all because of the expansion of iron in the heat. The iron structure of the Eiffel Tower expands in the summer's warmth and contracts in the winter's cold. So, it can change its height seasonally."

Josie's eyes widened as she covered her blooming cheeks. "That's incredible! So, the Eiffel Tower is like a living, breathing structure."

"I guess. It's one of those amazing wonders of science."

"Oh you and your science! It's in your bones!"

"Let me ask you this question, for scientific research," he raised his eyebrows and lifted his glass to his lips. "Have I stolen your heart yet?"

She cocked her head, her eyebrows raised, and her lips curved into a broad smile. "Well, Mr Quinn, you certainly have me intrigued."

As they finished their dessert, their conversation flowed naturally, infused with newfound knowledge and playfulness. They decided to continue their delightful evening with a stroll through the bustling mall. Their fingers entwined like two kindred spirits drawn together by an invisible force. Josie's breath hitched as a faint shiver coursed down her spine, a blend of anticipation and warmth. Her eyes met August's, finding a mirrored spark of surprise and an unspoken understanding. It was a simple touch, yet a universe of unspoken words bloomed between them. He flicked his eyes away, feeling heat rise up from his chest to his face.

"Hey, look, it's a piano!" He exclaimed, tearing away from her hand and throwing himself down on the bench.

Josie raised an eyebrow quizzically, "Do you know how to play?"

August chuckled, "No, but there's no harm in trying, is there? Come and sit with me!" His fingers danced over the keys, producing a whimsical medley of notes that reflected the playful spirit of the day. Josie, her heart echoing with joy, decided to join in. She set her hands on the keys, and batted his hands away. "Okay, move over. I can *actually* play."

August obliged, making room for her, his heart pounding with excitement as he wrapped an arm around her waist, watching as she placed her fingers on the keys, breathing softly as she played the opening chords of "The Parting Glass."

August's eyes softened as he recognised the tune. "I've not heard this song in ages!"

"You know this?"

August nodded.

"Seriously, what don't you know?"

His eyes sparkled with mirth, her fingers weaving the timeless melody. "Well, I don't think I could explain just how you managed to time travel 111 years into the future without theoretical physics being more than theoretical."

Her smile faded, and her eyebrows raised as she let out a bemused laugh. "Well, I suppose that's quite the mystery then, isn't it? Maybe I've just got a knack for defying the laws of physics. Or perhaps I stumbled upon a wormhole while playing this melody. Who knows?"

As their laughter and music intertwined, the mall's visitors paused in their hurried pace, drawn by the enchantment of an unexpected performance and the enduring magic of an improbable love story. She played the last few chords of the song, tuning into the people who were singing along to the music.

"Goodnight and joy be to you all!" Josie and August joined in as the chords faded into the soft hum of the mall's ambient noise. An applause took over the silence as August wrapped his arms tighter around her and Josie nestled her head on his shoulder, finding solace in the comforting rhythm of his heartbeat beneath her ear.

"Your girlfriend is good, sir!" An older man spoke, coming over from the bench he was sitting on to pat him on the back.

"She is, isn't she?"

Chapter Nine

Fields of Gold – Sting
31st March 1909, Belfast.

The gentle morning sun cast a warm glow over the cobblestone streets of Belfast, seeping through the lace curtains of the Melrose's home. It was a small building, adorned with polished wooden furniture, fine porcelain tea cups, and an air of nostalgia that whispered of generations past. The scent of freshly baked barmbrack hung in the air, while the creaking floors beneath their feet told stories of family life and shared experiences.

A fifteen year old girl stood in the doorway, her heart fluttering. She was going to work with her father. She wore a high-waisted linen dress, embellished with delicate lacework, and a wide-brimmed hat adorned with a silk ribbon that danced gently in the morning breeze. The hallway mirror reflected her youth, but her eyes, brimming with dreams, held wisdom.

Her mother, Róisín, busied herself in the kitchen, her hands trembling ever so slightly as she prepared sandwiches for their journey. The kitchen itself was a hub of family life, with an aged wooden table bearing the etchings of countless shared meals, and shelves filled with cherished recipe books passed down through generations. Róisín's loving eyes never wavered from her daughter, and her gaze held a blend of pride and the unspoken worry only a mother could carry. Josie offered a reassuring smile, tiptoeing as she waited for her father. Today, they were to witness history together, to be part of something monumental, and it filled her heart with both excitement and a touch of longing.

"Are you absolutely sure you want to go, Josie, my dear? You don't have to go if you don't want to." Róisín asked, packing a sandwich into her satchel. Josie nodded resolutely, her determination shining through her gaze. "I'll be fine, Mum. Dad will make sure I'm safe. This is a once-in-a-lifetime opportunity. I must see the keel being laid. Who knows when such a chance will come again?"

Róisín sighed, her love for her daughter radiating in her soft green eyes. Her hand found its way to Josie's shoulder, a gesture of both affection and a plea for caution. "I understand, but I can't help but worry. Promise me that you'll be careful. Don't get too close to the riveters. Wrought Iron rivets are very hot."

"I promise," Josie assured, enfolding her mother in a warm hug. "We'll be back before you know it." Her father, Michael, walked in the room, a smile playing on his lips as he swung his bag over his shoulder. "Come along, Josie. We better head off now if we want to make it in time."

He leant over to Róisín and brought her in for a hug.

"Don't let her get hurt." Róisín warned, her index finger waving in the air.

"I wouldn't dream of it. I love you Róisín." Michael kissed her cheek and took Josie's hand, beaming at her.

Their journey took them through the bustling streets of Belfast, a city steeped in tradition and brimming with history. It was a place where horse-drawn carriages shared the cobbled road with early cars, and daily life was a tapestry of hard work and enduring customs. Josie and Michael approached the shipyard's grand entrance, their hearts swelled with anticipation. Josie's eyes darted to the hum of industrious workers, the grandeur of the gantries and her father. The cold air of the morning seeped into her cheeks as she took in the sight in front of her. Michael leaned in, his voice a soothing murmur, as he whispered, "You are witnessing living history. Cherish this moment. You have but one life to make the most of this world. Just one, Josie. Josie?"

***

"Josie!" A voice weaved through the remnants of her dream and she sat up. "Dad?"

"No, Josie, it's August. I think you were dreaming," he replied softly, his voice a lifeline to the present. The remnants of her dream began to dissipate, leaving behind a heavy ache in her heart. Unwanted tears welled up in her eyes, glistening with unspoken sadness as she anxiously chewed her lower lip between her teeth.

"I'm sorry, Josie."

"No—" Her eyes darted around, panic rising in her cheeks as she fumbled for something to ground herself. Her fingers found the blanket and she rolled her thumb across the knots.

"Do you want a hug?"

She pressed her lips in a hard line and nodded. His eyes softened as he shuffled across to her on the bed and enveloped her in his arms, drawing her close to shield her from the ache of her yearning. He rubbed her back as she buried herself into his shoulder, her tears flowing silently.

"I was only supposed to have one life to make the most of the world."

"Who told you that?"

"My father. He took me to watch the keel being laid. I shouldn't be here."

"But I'm so glad you are. You make me so happy, Josephine." He wiped her tears from her sodden cheeks with the pad of his thumbs. "Sometimes one life isn't enough to experience everything."

"But why me!" She yelled, her eyes wide and her lips trembling. "Why me, August? Why not my parents?"

"I don't know why. I don't know all of the answers. This is something even the best scientist would struggle to explain. But you know what? Your parents, they would be proud of the person you've become. Their love lives on in you, in your heart, and it's a beautiful legacy to carry with you. You're so strong, Josie. *So strong.* I'm so amazed at how well you're dealing with this world, this second chance you're living. I— I don't think I'd be strong enough."

"Yes you would."

"*No*, I wouldn't. Josie, sweetheart, you don't give yourself enough credit."

"They're dead and I'm sitting here crying, I'm not strong." Josie took a shaky breath, her eyes still shimmering with unshed tears, but her gaze unwavering as she met August's compassionate eyes. His smile softened, and he reached out to gently wipe away a new tear that had escaped her eye. "Josie, letting yourself feel, allowing yourself to cry, that's not a sign of weakness. It's a testament to your humanity. Grief is a part of life, and it's okay to mourn."

"I don't know what I'd do without you, August. I—" Their bodies pressed together, as if he could shield her against the pain of the world. With her head on his chest, she extended her arm to move the blanket around her. She draped it over their shoulders, cocooning them in its comforting embrace.

"C-Can I ask something?"

"Of course," August replied, his eyes attentive.

"Did you mind that man calling me your girlfriend yesterday?" She asked, her curiosity tinged with a hint of insecurity. August's smile grew, and he gently brushed a strand of hair from her face. "Well, it's not every day a stranger thinks I am with the most beautiful girl on the planet."

A soft blush graced Josie's cheeks at his words, and she couldn't help but smile. In that moment, the weight of her past, and the longing for her parents, seemed a bit lighter.

***

Walking hand in hand through Runyon Canyon Park, the late afternoon sun bathed the landscape in a golden hue. The wind whispered through the trees, rustling their leaves and teasing Josie's hair. It was a moment of tranquillity and connection, their steps in harmony with the gentle sway of the branches above. Josie's thoughts were her silent companions as they strolled along the trail. The weight of her memories tugged at her, and a pang of sadness weaved into the beat of her heart.

"What are you thinking about?"

A sombre smile graced Josie's lips as she confessed, "My parents. I'm sorry." They came to a standstill beneath the generous shade of an old oak tree. Its branches swayed gently in the breeze, sharing in the quiet moment between the two of them. Josie's eyes shimmered with unshed tears, and she leaned into August's comforting presence, looking at the long grass swaying underfoot.

"Don't apologise, I understand," August reassured her, his voice soft and full of empathy. He gently tucked a stray hair that had escaped from behind her ear, his touch as tender as his words.

"I've got something that will cheer you up, though—a surprise."

"What is it?"

"Tomorrow," A toothy grin played on his lips. "I'm taking you on a plane."

Tears of sadness were replaced by tears of joy as Josie's eyes widened with excitement. "What? How? Don't tell me you're a qualified— air captain?" Her pulse quickened, the rush of adrenaline surging through her veins. August chuckled, his eyes twinkling with mischief. "No, no, I'm not a pilot. We will have the first lesson, and we can choose to carry on if we want."

"So, we're actually going up in a flying machine... an aeroplane?"

August's grin was infectious, and he couldn't contain his own excitement. "Yep."

She squealed with delight and jumped into his arms. Her laughter, as melodious as a songbird's serenade, echoed through the park, filling every nook and cranny with her elation. August spun her around, their laughter blending with the gentle caress of the wind.

"I'm so happy I could kiss you! Thank you!" She exclaimed, her eyes shining with pure delight.

"Kiss me then," August invited, his eyes brimming with warmth and affection. Josie's heart, though eager, held a moment of hesitation, a fluttering of emotions that only intensified her longing. Her lips parted as she leant into him, and their lips met in a gentle, lingering kiss. The world around them faded as their connection deepened, and the warmth of their affection radiated like the sun's final, golden embrace before it set. It was a promise, silent yet profound. Their kiss deepened, each moment stretching into eternity as they lost themselves in the warmth of their affection. Josie's hands found their way into August's hair, her fingers gently tangling in its soft strands, while August's arms held her close, preventing her from ever feeling the pull of the ground.

When they finally, reluctantly, pulled apart, their eyes locked in a mesmerising gaze. The world around them ceased to exist as they watched each other, the silence between them filled with an unspoken promise of the love that had taken root in their hearts. Their souls had woven together in a way that words could never capture, and in that shared look, they found a world of understanding and adoration that left them both breathless.

"Was that alright?"

"Perfect." Josie whispered, leaning in for another kiss.

Chapter Ten

Just Like Heaven – The Cure

August and Josie stood beside the small aircraft on the tarmac. The moment had finally arrived. The setting sun bathed everything in a warm and golden hue, making the plane before them shine like a jewel in the fading light. Its wings stretched wide, ready to take flight, and it looked like a dream come true. Josie adjusted her cap with a grin, her fingers tracing its worn edges as she beamed at August, her excitement palpable in the rosy glow of her cheeks.

"You know, pilots don't wear these anymore."

"Well I do!"

August watched her with adoration, the smile on his face growing with each moment that passed. Her excitement was infectious, and he couldn't help but be swept up in her enthusiasm. They were about to fly, to live a dream she had carried from her time, and it was a moment that he was thrilled to share with her. As they settled into the small aircraft, the pilot, Captain Reynolds, turned to Josie and August, a glint of excitement in his eyes. "Welcome aboard, folks. August and Josie right?"

"Yes, sir." August smiled, shaking his hand.

"Great. Nice to meet you both. Are you ready for your flying lesson?"

Josie nodded eagerly, her eyes filled with anticipation. "Yes, sir. We can't wait. And are you Irish by chance?"

Captain Reynolds beamed. "Yes, I am! Westport. RoI"

"RoI?"

"Republic of Ireland," Captain Reynolds explained. "It's what we call the southern part of Ireland. It was split in 1921 into Northern Ireland and the Republic of Ireland. Surely you know that?"

"Oh yes, I did. I've just never heard it be shortened to RoI. Sorry. I'm from Belfast, Northern Ireland." She smiled, trying out the new name.

Captain Reynolds smiled warmly, "No need to apologise. It's always nice to meet fellow Irish folks. Ready to learn how to fly?"

"Absolutely." August beamed, gripping Josie's hand.

"Alright, first things first. This plane is a Cessna 172 Skyhawk. She can make a max speed of 163 knots, but her cruising speed is 122 knots. This here," he gestured to a control stick, "is the yoke. It's what you'll use to control the pitch of the aircraft, making it climb or descend. Push forward to go down, pull back to go up. These pedals down here, they control the rudder. That helps steer the plane left or right, port or starboard. Your feet will come into play when you need to turn."

"The rudder? Like on ships?"

"Exactly." Reynolds smiled, turning to August. "She knows her stuff"

"She likes to learn, don't you Josie?"

Josie nodded enthusiastically, her heart swelling with a sense of accomplishment.

"It's a good quality to have." The pilot's enthusiasm was infectious. "And these levers control the throttle. Push them forward to increase speed, pull them back to slow down. It's like the gas pedal in your car."

"I'm afraid I know nothing about cars, captain."

"No worries, Josie. We'll go through more as we fly, but these are the essentials to get you started. Ready to take the yoke?"

"What, me?" Josie's face lit up with excitement as she nodded, her fingers itching to grasp the yoke. "Absolutely, I'm ready!"

"Great, go ahead and put on these headphones," he instructed with a reassuring smile. "They'll allow you to hear me through them, and I should be able to hear you. There's a microphone, too. Give it a try."

Josie studied the headphones, her eyes widening with curiosity. "The microphone?" she whispered, her fingers hovering over the small, cylindrical device. August nodded, encouraging her. "That's right, Josie. This," he pointed to the microphone, "is the mic. Just say something simple like 'testing 1, 2, 3' to check if it's working."

Josie cleared her throat, a hint of excitement in her voice. "This is Captain Melrose. Testing 1, 2, 3." Her words flowed through the microphone, and she could hear her voice resonating through the headphones.

"Alright, Captain Melrose," the captain said, his voice calm and reassuring as he let out a soft chuckle. "Let's get this beauty off the ground."

The engine roared to life, and Josie taxied to the runway.

"Just steer slowly, keep the nose straight ahead..." Josie's grip on the yoke tightened, and she looked over at August, her eyes filled with a mix of excitement and a hint of nervousness. August smiled and squeezed her hand.

"It's okay, don't panic. It's safe."

"I'm not. I know it is."

"Now... pull the yoke towards you and we'll go up." With a gradual burst of speed, the plane took off smoothly, and the sensation of flight was exhilarating. The world fell away beneath them as they climbed higher into the sky. Josie's eyes widened, and she let out a joyful laugh that mingled with the wind rushing past the plane's windows.

"Now, August, this is the altimeter. It's kind of like a clock. The long hand moves in intervals of 10,000, the shorter hand moves in intervals of 1000, and the middle has intervals of 100. And this is an ASI — Airspeed indicator. It's simple to read. The hand is how many knots we're making. Can you tell me our altitude and our speed, please."

"We're going at 122 knots, altitude of 13,500 feet, right?"

"Nice work!" Captain Reynolds cheered. "Just level the yoke, Josie, this is cruising altitude."

"How does this work?"

"Well the wings are designed to create lift when air flows over and under them. It allows them to stay in the air and move forward. These control the plane's direction and stability using different control surfaces." August explained, a smirk tugging the corners of his lips.

"You're such a show off."

"You asked!"

"The captain, not you!"

They soared through the air, and the view of the city below was breathtaking. The streets and buildings became smaller and smaller, like a miniature cityscape. Josie's laughter continued, a melodic soundtrack to their journey. It was the sound of pure joy, and August couldn't help but be enchanted by it. As the small aircraft soared through the clear blue sky, August's eyes met Josie's, a playful glint in his gaze. Then, with a soft and melodious voice, he began to sing, his words carrying a wealth of emotion.

"Come, Josephine, in my flying machine..."

Josie's heart skipped a beat as the lyrics reached her ears. She felt a rush of emotion, a connection to a past she had thought was forever lost. August's voice, wrapped around her like a gentle caress, and the world around them seemed to disappear. It was just the two of them, suspended in the sky, sharing a moment that transcended time.

"And it's up she goes! Up she goes! Balance yourself like a bird on a beam, in the air she goes! There she goes!" Tears welled up in her eyes as she listened to the lyrics, and reached for August's hand, their fingers intertwining, grounding her in the present, yet connecting her to the past. August's singing filled the plane with warmth and love. It was as though the song had become a bridge between their worlds, a reminder of the depth of their connection.

"It's your song, Josie." August leaned over and pressed a tender kiss to her cheek, his voice soft and filled with affection. A silent laugh escaped her lips as she pushed the pedal, turning the plane to port.

"God, I've not heard that song in years!" The captain's voice crackled into the silence as he took over the yoke. "Where did you learn it?"

Josie's attention shifted to the captain's voice, but her gaze moved back up to fix on August. Her voice wavered as she tried to reply, her words filled with emotion. "It's just a song I, uh, p-picked up." She continued to watch August, her eyes locked with his, as if the world around them had faded into the background. The connection they shared, the unspoken emotions, were more powerful than any words. It was a moment of pure, unadulterated happiness, a memory that they would cherish for the rest of their lives. In the cockpit of the small aircraft, among the clouds and the setting sun, they were free, and their love felt boundless.

***

The night sky stretched above them from the rooftop that evening, a celestial canvas painted with stars. A telescope stood beside them, its lens pointed towards space, offering a glimpse into the mysteries of the universe. Soft music played in the background from his phone, its gentle melodies creating a harmonious backdrop to the mesmerising celestial display. The twinkling stars mirrored in Josie's eyes, and the telescope's presence was a portal to a world beyond.

Josie, her eyes filled with wonder, had kicked off her shoes, and her frilly white ankle socks peeked out from beneath the hem of her dress as she tiptoed towards the telescope. The city lights shimmered around her, stretching out before her, a dazzling array of colours and motion.

August followed her, taking her hand in his. "Can I ask you something, Josie?"

"Of course."

"Do you ever wish to go back to your time?"

Josie gazed at the stars above, her eyes shimmering with the reflections of a thousand galaxies. Her thoughts were a constellation of emotions as flattened her feet on the cool ground and puffed her cheeks. "Part of me misses the simplicity of my time, the familiar faces, and the places I grew up with. But another part of me has grown fond of this world, and of you, August." She turned to face him, her gaze a reflection of the universe's vastness. Her lips curved into a soft smile, as she drew her body closer to his, moving her hands to the nape of his neck.

"I love you." His mouth dropped open as a wave of surprise and delight washed over him. He smiled shyly, his heart racing with joy.

"You have no idea how long I've been waiting to hear you say that, Josie."

She tiptoed to meet him, her movements a celestial dance as she wrapped his arms around his neck to meet him in a passionate kiss. The rooftop around them was a silent witness to the beauty of their connection, and the city below seemed to twinkle in celebration. She wrapped her arms around his neck and pressed herself into him, feeling his arms wrap around her waist. When they pulled away, Josie looked up at him with a loving smile, her cheeks glowing. "You know so much about me."

August smiled, his eyes filled with warmth and adoration as his golden hair billowed around their faces. "I like—"

"You like to learn."

August chuckled and kissed her cheek. "No, sweetheart, I like to learn about things I love. And I love you."

Josie's heart swelled with affection, and she hugged him tightly. The night air around them was filled with a sense of contentment, as if the universe itself had aligned to bring them together.

"August?"

"Yes, Josie?"

"What's this song?"

"Just like Heaven. It's quite fitting, don't you think?"

"Why?"

"This moment with you is just like heaven. You're ethereal, Josie." He whispered, his words filled with tenderness. Josie gazed into his eyes, her voice soft and filled with emotion.

The night deepened around them, the city below shimmering like a sea of stars. They sat on the rooftop, holding each other close, their hearts connected to the vastness of the universe. They watched the stars dance through the heavens, their souls dancing among the constellations, united by a love that was truly out of this world.

Chapter Eleven

Mo Ghile Mear – Órla Fallon

Wrapped in the gentle, amber glow of a salt lamp, August and Josie lay tangled together beneath their shared blanket. The room was transformed into an ethereal sanctuary, where time and space seemed to fade, leaving them cocooned in the warmth of their affection.

"I love this blanket so much," Josie whispered, her voice filled with tenderness, as her fingers danced reverently over the soft fabric. "It's so cosy and comforting. Like a hug from the past."

August met her gaze with a bright smile, but his eyes were dull. He clung to the blanket. "Yeah, it is." She shifted closer to August, her head in the crook of his neck, and reached out to brush a strand of hair from his forehead.

"Your mother made it didn't she?"

August hummed, his body stiffening as she stroked his hair. "Can you tell me about her? How did she... um—"

"Die?" August's fingers stilled their gentle exploration on the blanket, and he inhaled deeply, the memories of his past pressing upon him. "Cancer. I was nineteen. Liv was fifteen."

Her eyes softened, and she leaned in closer, her voice a soothing balm. She tucked a loose strand of hair behind his ear, her fingers lingering on his skin. "That must have been so hard," her words were a gentle caress.

"It was," August admitted, his voice quivering with emotion. His eyes welled up with tears, and he swallowed to keep them at bay. "Cancer is the worst fucking thing ever," he said, his words trembling with the weight of painful memories. "It really sucks seeing someone so ill." His voice was filled with a raw, unspoken anguish, shaking as he recalled all the memories. He swallowed the lump in the base of his throat. "During her treatment, my dad turned to alcohol and was rarely home. I had to quit doing the things I loved to do to look after Liv, and it sounds selfish but it was hard."

Josie moved up on her pillow, holding him to her chest as he wrapped an arm around her waist.

"Was playing the guitar one of the things you used to love doing?"

He nodded. "I was in a band... I was the lead guitarist, and... I gave it all up. I looked after everyone when no one else could."

"Oh, *mo ghile mear*, you were so strong. You still are." She took his face in her hands, wiping away hot tears that had tracked down his cheeks, her eyes soft with affection. "N-no, Josie, I wasn't. I nearly turned to alcohol too." Her hand found his, and their fingers intertwined, resting on the blanket.

"But you didn't," Josie whispered, her voice soft and filled with a deep affection. Their closeness was palpable, as if they were two hearts beating in unison. August shook his head, his vulnerability laid bare. "No. For Liv's sake. She deserved better. I promised myself I would never drink away my problems."

"What happened to your father? I mean is he still—"

"He's better now," August replied, "but he never likes to talk about Mom, or what happened. We don't talk about feelings with him. We can't... not anymore."

She nodded in understanding and leaned in to press a kiss into his hair. "How do *you* feel about it?"

"I... I need to talk about her, to get my feelings out," August confessed, his voice laden with the weight of his history. "That's why the blanket is so comforting. It's the only thing I have left to remember her by... because my father acts like she never existed."

"Why did you let me use it if it means this much to you?"

He ran his thumb over her hand. "It helped me through a hard time. I thought it could help you too. Can we talk about something more cheerful now?"

She smiled, her gaze dropping to the blanket. Her head remained on his shoulder, and she pressed a soft kiss to his cheek. "Sure. Anything you like."

"What was that thing you said in Irish?" August asked, curiosity brightening his eyes.

"Mo ghile mear," Josie whispered. Her lips were inches from his, and they shared a brief, tender kiss, his fingers cupping her chin as hers tangled in his hair. "My gallant star."

Her eyes searched his, and a smile tugged at the corner of her mouth. "You're so brave, August. Believe it." She whispered it against his mouth before claiming another soft kiss, her eyes closed. A warm smile tugged at the corners of August's lips as she pulled away.

"Can you write that down for me? I ought to get that tattooed."

"Yes, of course." Josie sat up, reaching into her bedside table and pulling out a pen and August's notebook. She placed it on her knee and opened it, poising her pen above the page.

"I've got a better one that we could both get tattooed."

"What's that?"

"*Gan am.* Timeless."

"It's so beautiful," August said, his eyes locking with Josie's, their gazes filled with longing. Write them both down for me, on separate pages."

"Of course," Josie replied, beaming. "I'm going to add an extra bit on the first one."

"Sure."

" Is breá liom tú, mo ghile mear. "

~ Josie ♡

and,

"Táimid gan am ."

"What does is breá liom mean?"

She flicked her eyes between his eyes and his lips, and placed her hands on either side of his neck. "I love you." She pressed her lips to his, and moved back down to his shoulder, wrapping the blanket back around their bodies.

***

It was a bright, busy day, a stark contrast to the intimate sanctuary of their bedroom. As they strolled, August held Josie's hand, just below her fresh tattoo. The streets were alive with the symphony of urban life, with people rushing to their destinations, the aroma of street food wafting through the air, and the chatter of conversations blending into a harmonious cacophony. August and Josie navigated through the throngs of people, their closeness palpable, their fingers tracing the fresh ink on each other's skin whenever they could.

"I wish I knew how to speak Irish."

"Well, English became the dominant language in the 19th century, so you're fine," Josie assured him, their fingers interlaced, holding each other close.

"I know," August said, his fingers tracing the lines of her tattoo. "But it's so pretty, Josie!"

"Yes, but the phonics are a bitch." As they continued down the bustling street, their tattoos fresh and their hearts overflowing with affection, they couldn't help but smile at each other. Josie reached out to touch the ink on August's arm, her fingers tracing the lines of the tattoo.

"Does your tattoo hurt?"

"A little," August admitted, his eyes locked onto hers. "Does yours?" Josie's smile was radiant. "Yes. But it was worth it."

"Was it worth the 111-year temporal leap?"

Josie's smile widened, and she tightened her grip on his hand, pulling him closer. "Absolutely."

Chapter Twelve

Summer Night City– ABBA

The room was cosy, their tired laughter and conversations echoing off the walls. It was a tranquil space, filled with the soft glow of moonlight spilled in through the window, inviting hues across the room, setting a serene atmosphere. She sat on his lap, her arm around his shoulders as he wrapped his around her waist, smiling as they showed their wrists to the computer

"You got matching tattoos?" Liv's voice burst through the screen. "And didn't invite me?"

August and Josie exchanged a knowing look, their smiles revealing a shared secret. Their fingers intertwined, drawing them closer as they shared their special news.

"Well it's kind of a personal thing." Josie laughed, lowering her wrist.

"What does it say?" Liv's curiosity was insatiable, her voice like a melody that harmonised with their own.

"*Táimid gan am,*" August replied, his voice carrying a hint of playful mischief.

Liv sighed, burying her head in her hands. "August, I don't have time for your games. What does it say?"

Josie's laughter danced in the air as she leaned in closer to the computer. "It's Irish. It means 'We're timeless.' Good pronunciation, by the way, *mo ghile mear.*" she added with a wink.

"Mo..." her voice trailed off. "So you're learning Irish now? What does *that* mean?"

"My gallant star." August explained, softening his eyes. "I told her about mom and dad."

"Oh." Liv breathed, looking down to her fingers. "Are you okay?"

"Yeah." August wrapped his arm back around Josie and leaned into the chair. "It's better that she knows, Liv."

"Oh, so you're *actually* together now?"

"Yep." August's grin radiated across the screen, as if his happiness filled the room, every corner touched by the warmth of his smile. He wrapped an arm around her shoulder and rubbed it. "Josie's stuck with me now!"

Liv laughed, her melodious voice joining the chorus of affection. "I wouldn't like to rip you from your boyfriend," she playfully teased, her voice filled with warmth. "But I'm sure there are some modern things this muppet has failed to show you."

August sighed dramatically, throwing his head back against the back of his chair and sliding his hand down his face.

"Right. What's the OKQP?"

Josie's brow furrowed as she turned to him, mouthing. "What's OKQP"

"Olivia Kate Quinn Plan. Noun: a plan which *will* result in adverse effects." August chuckled, hiding his grin in Josie's hair.

"No it won't! Do you want to know what the plan is or not?"

"Go on." August sighed.

"Six Flags!"

"What's that?"

Liv beamed, her face aching with a forming smile. "It's a theme park in Valencia."

Josie's eyes widened, as she flickered her eyes across August's face. "Spain? Isn't that far from here?"

"No, sweetheart, Valencia, California. It won't take long to drive."

Liv's face glowed with excitement, "It has loads of roller coasters, rides, and games. You'll love it!" Her words were like a radiant burst of energy, igniting the room with the promise of thrilling escapades and endless fun.

"Well *finally*, there is something you've come up with that isn't bound to be a total disaster!" August snorted playfully.

"Thanks. I'm coming round right now. Pack a small bag, and I'll pick you up in 20!" Her words were an invitation to an unforgettable day, and she hung up the call.

"Well, I guess that's our plans sorted for the day."

"I guess." Josie laughed, leaning into him and pressing her lips against his.

***

Liv's car was filled with laughter as they made their way down the winding roads, each thread of the sky tinged with the golden hues of a California summer. Music graced the car's interior, its notes dancing like fireflies, painting the air with a melody that whispered of bygone days.

"What's this song called?" Josie inquired, cradling August's phone with a newfound confidence. "I'm going to add it to our playlist."

"Summer Night City by ABBA," August replied, a subtle pride in his voice.

"ABBA?" Josie intonated, her eyebrows furrowing. "That's an interesting name. Who is that?"

"They're a band from Sweden," Liv explained with a knowing smile. "It's an acronym for their names: Anni-Frid, Benny, Björn, and Agnetha."

Josie's eyes sparkled. "That's clever! Do they make good music? Well they must because... this is brilliant!"

"Arguably the best."

The music wafted through the vehicle, an enchanting atmosphere enveloped them—a sweet nostalgia that lingered like the fragrance of summer blooms. In that car, beneath the azure sky, the air hummed with the poetry of summer's past, and every laughter-filled mile carried them deeper into the embrace of cherished memories. As Liv parked, the sprawling theme park came into view, its towering rides rising into the sky like giants of steel and colour. The vibrant hues of the park's attractions painted a vivid landscape, and the air was thick with the exhilarating scent of adventure. Josie's eyes widened in awe as they checked in and received their wristbands. The atmosphere around the park was electric, like a buzzing energy that filled the air with excitement and anticipation.

Her anticipation was tinged with a hint of apprehension as she watched the roller coasters loop and twist through the sky. August reached her side, his fingers gently squeezing her hand. "Don't worry, sweetheart. All of the rides are tested daily. They're very safe."

"Promise?"

He smiled, cupping her face. "I won't let anything happen to you."

She nodded, taking a deep breath and walked towards the first ride with Liv. As they were secured into their seats, her heart raced, and a sense of exhilaration washed over her. She clung to Liv's hand, her laughter mingling with the screams of excitement as the coaster soared through the twists and turns, the world blurring around her. From the ground, August watched with a mix of amusement and adoration. He couldn't take his eyes off her, and each moment of the ride was etched into his memory. He watched as her blurred, spinning face lit up with pure joy, her distant laughter like music to his ears. It was a song that their playlist could never compare to. When the ride came to an end, Josie stumbled as she stepped off the platform, and her legs felt like jelly.

August was there to catch her, his arms wrapping around her. "Looks like you had fun," he said with a warm smile, his fingers ruffling her hair gently.

"Mhm, I feel like I'm orbiting space." Josie leaned into him, her head resting on his shoulder. "It was amazing. Thank you."

"Do you need some water?" Liv asked, reaching into her bag, producing a bottle of water, and handing it to her.

"Please. Thank you."

They walked away from the ride, Liv and August holding one of Josie's hands each. In the enchanting landscape of the theme park, they moved with the effortless grace of carefree teenagers. weaving through the vibrant tapestry of attractions. Their laughter, a cascade of jubilant notes, painted the air with hues of joy.

"Josie, look, a trampoline!"

"A what?"

"A trampoline! It's like a, um, a springboard." Liv explained. "Come on, you'll love it!"

With a tentative nod, Josie took a small step onto the trampoline, her grip on their hands tight. The surface felt foreign beneath her feet, and a delicate uncertainty played on her features. Liv bounced lightly to demonstrate, the springs responding with a playful rebound.

"See? Easy peasy!"

Josie's movements were a symphony of joy, each jump becoming freer than the last, and her smile widened until it ached to do so. Their hands entwined, they jumped, soaring into the clouds. Breathless yet curious, Josie turned to August, a playful gleam in her eyes. "How does this work?"

"When you jump on a trampoline, your weight compresses the springs, transferring kinetic energy to them. Hooke's Law comes into play—force is directly proportional to the distance the springs are compressed. Essentially, the harder you jump, the higher you'll bounce, thanks to the springs reacting with equal force in the opposite direction. It's a bit like Newton's third law—equal and opposite reactions."

Liv scoffed. "Showoff."

"Eejit. Seriously, how do you know everything?"

With a bashful grin, August replied, "Well, almost *everything*. There's still one mystery I can't crack."

"What's that?"

"How did you time travel?"

Their bouncing slowed, and in that gentle descent, August locked eyes with Josie, gripping her hand. "You know what? It doesn't matter how you got here, I'm just grateful you are."

He leaned in, placing his hand in her neck, and placing his thumb on her chin, leaning in, and sharing a soft, lingering kiss—a promise sealed. He tucked a strand of her auburn hair behind her ear and wrapped an arm around her shoulder.

"Ew, get a room! And come on! I want to get slushies!" Josie and August laughed, bouncing off the trampoline and joining Liv's side.

As they approached the slushie stand, the colourful array of frozen delights beckoned. Josie's eyes widened, taking in the swirling machines. "What's the big deal with slushies, anyway?"

"They're like a burst of frozen happiness in your mouth. You'll see."

Just as Josie was about to make her flavour selection, she hesitated and then, with a shy yet excited smile, announced, "You know, it's my birthday tomorrow."

Liv's eyes lit up with surprise and delight, "Really? Well then, consider this a pre-birthday celebration!"

August chuckled, accepting his blue raspberry slushie. "I know, Josie. Tomorrow is going to be unforgettable." He winked, the warmth in his gaze held a promise of joy yet to unfold.

"Yeah, maybe he might get his guitar out for the first time in forever."

"Don't push your luck, Olivia." He darted his eyes to Josie, a sad glimmer reflecting in the flecks of light within his irises.

"I can't wait either way. There's no pressure, mo ghile mear." Josie whispered, squeezing his hand and looking over to the woman standing behind the slushie stand. "Hi, I'll take the strawberry kiwi please."

Chapter Thirteen

Wings– Birdy

The first light of morning tiptoed into the room with the grace of a delicate ballet, illuminated by the soft orange glow of a candle. At the foot of the bed, Liv and August, silhouetted by the soft hues of dawn, held a small cake adorned with a solitary, flickering candle. August sat on the edge of the bed, his fingers gently caressing the strings of his guitar, and Josie watched, her head resting back on the pillows as her eyes glistened with tears.

"Happy birthday, dear Josieeeee! Happy birthday to you!" August closed his eyes, his hands stilling on the strings. For a moment, the room seemed suspended in time, filled only with the echoes of his music and the quiet solace it brought. Then, slowly, he opened his eyes, his gaze finding Josie's across the room, watching as she held her hand to her mouth, tears spilling down her face. His hand drifted across the fretboard, and it squeaked, as he propped it against the wall.

"What's wrong?"

She sniffed. "You're playing the guitar. You've not played the guitar since..."

"I know," he nodded, squeezing her hands, and swallowing. "I wanted to show you something special for your birthday." Their eyes met, tracing each line of each other's faces. Her eyes were wide, filled with childlike wonder. "Now, make a wish, eejit."

She sat up and blew the candle out, a tender bloom in her chest. August leaned down, enveloping her in a cocoon of morning warmth, and she wrapped her arms around his neck, her fingers gently entwined in the tousled strands of his hair.

"Time to get up," August whispered, his breath a soft caress against her ear. He moved over to the window and opened the blinds. "We're going out."

"Where?"

"It's a surprise!" Liv exclaimed, her eyes dancing with excitement. "Get dressed and join us in the kitchen for some cake!" With a gleeful giggle, she dashed out, plate in hand. August had a grin playing on his lips as he waved to Josie before following Liv, a playful twinkle in his eyes.

***

"You really want to know, hm?" August teased, reaching into his glove box.

"Yes, I do."

"Here's a map of California. Look for Temecula."

"Temecula? That's such a strange name."

"Oh, what and Ballyshannon isn't?"

"Actually." Josie looked up, a grin tugging her lips across her face. "Baile na is Irish for Place of. What's your excuse?"

His mouth widened into a smile, and she sighed, running a hand down her face. "Oh god. You've got a fact haven't you?"

"The word Temecula comes from the Luiseño Indian word Temecunga. Temet means sun, and -ngna means place of."

"Is everyday gonna be a language and etymology lesson with you two?" Liv laughed. "Ooh! Look outside Josie!"

She turned her head, casting her eyes up towards the sky, her mouth widening into a smile. Vibrant hues of hot air balloons painted the sky, a celestial palette that beckoned them to ascend into the clouds.

"Surprise." He whispered. "Happy birthday."

"Are we going up in one of those... blimps?"

"They're hot air balloons." He turned the car off and took her hand in his, helping her out of the car. "And yes, if you want to." She flicked her eyes between his, and stole a kiss from his lips, her arms wrapping around his neck. Liv clicked a button on her camera and beamed at them as they pulled away from each other, their eyebrows raised.

"Photography project," she explained, lowering the camera into a bag by her side. "You don't mind, do you?"

"No," Josie whispered, drawing closer to her. "Is that what cameras look like now? Wow they're so... unclunky."

"Uncluncky?"

"Is that not a word?"

August wrapped his arms around her, holding back a chuckle. "Come on. We want to get up in the air *today*, don't we?"

***

The eager caress of warm brush strokes painted a soft summer sky behind them as their balloon floated higher, transforming the sky into a mesmerising canvas. The once expansive landscape below gradually shrank, with the land diminishing into miniature details, behind the wispy clouds which danced around them.

"The world is so beautiful from up here." August observed, watching a bird swoop across the valleys.

"Almost picture worthy." Liv added. "Can I get another of you two?"

Josie nodded, pulling herself away from the corner of the basket and towards August's corner. "What do you need us to do?"

"Anything. Let the wind carry the story in your eyes," Liv directed, closing one and positioning the camera in front of her. August cradled Josie's face in his hands, and the camera shutter snapped, freezing their love in a single frame.

"Great, another! Let's get some natural smiles," she bent her knees, closing one eye, and squinting into the camera. "August, say something...nice."

Josie's eyes illuminated as she spread her arms in the open expanse of the sky, her head tilted back and her eyes gently closed. He smiled, his eyes brimming with soft tears. "You are the poetry written in the language of the skies," He whispered, his words a soft sonnet to the woman who had become the muse of his heart. Josie blushed, a rosy hue painting her cheeks, an echo of dawn's tender glow, and opened her eyes, turning to face him.

"You're so poetic."

Snap! Snap! Snap!

"I think I've got enough photos to make a picture book about you both now." Liv laughed, putting her camera away. "Thank you."

"Well, you better get an A on this project, Olivia, or I'm gonna—"

"You're gonna what?" She snickered. "Throw me out of a 737?"

"Better. An A380."

"Why an A380?"

"They're the fastest passenger plane." Josie explained.

"How fast?"

"About 511 knots, give or take, right August?" She looked at him, watching his lips curve upwards into a proud smile.

" Wow, sorry I asked," Liv scoffed. "I'll make sure to get an A. I don't want your smart arses coming after me."

Josie drifted back over to the corner, her eyes glazed as she watched the world pass by. August, his heart heavy with anticipation, reached into his pocket.

"Liv, camera," he mouthed urgently, motioning for her attention. Liv quickly readied her camera, her hands shaking with anticipation. He stepped towards her, brushing an arm around her waist, tapping her shoulder gently. His heart pounded in his chest as he opened his mouth to whisper her name, August tapped her shoulder gently, his heart pounding in his chest. But before he could utter a word, her hand drifted to her head and she swayed to the side, exhaling sharply as she fought to hold herself up.

"Josie, hey, are you okay?" August asked, his eyebrows furrowed, as he shoved the box back into his pocket, pursing his lips.

Josie's eyes fluttered open, her gaze meeting August's with a mix of confusion and discomfort. "I... I don't feel well," she murmured, her voice barely audible. August's heart sank as he watched Josie's distress, his own emotions swirling with worry and fear. He covered his mouth with the back of his hand and exchanged a glance with Liv, their eyes wide.

"Let's get you home then," August said softly, turning his eyes to the pilot, and smiling. "Can we get down please, sir?"

"No problem. There's some bottled water if you would like to drink it, Miss Melrose, but please don't sit. It's not safe."

"Thank you." Josie leaned against August, her breathing laboured and her eyes closed, as she slowly sipped the water, holding her hand over August's as he pressed it to her lips.

"We're descending now, Josie. How bad is it?"

"Do you remember when I went on that... ride yesterday?" August nodded cautiously, feeling her arm tighten around his neck. "It's a lot worse than that." He looked at her, noticing her face paling, and her body swaying slightly, and exchanged another fearful glance with Liv.

The descent of the hot air balloon brought a subtle unease to August's face, and in the car, his eyes remained flicked between the road and Josie, who was sprawled across the backseat, her usual effervescence tempered by a quiet weariness. Liv, sensing the shift, furrowed her brows, exchanging glances with August in the rearview mirror. Arriving home, Josie was disoriented, her temperature rising like a feverish dream. August maintained a reassuring smile—a façade for Liv and Josie's sake. In the tranquillity of their home, he guided Josie to bed with a tenderness that betrayed his concern.

"August, what's going on?" Liv whispered, concern etched across her face as she watched him take the seat opposite her. "She was perfectly fine up until—-"

"I... I'm not sure. Maybe the excitement caught up to her. She'll be fine," August smiled, though the uncertainty lingered in his eyes. Liv nodded, not entirely convinced, and offered a comforting touch on his arm. "If you need anything, let me know. And don't feel like you need to protect me again. I can cope."

His eyes flickered across hers, sensing the shift from the youthful innocence he was used to to a maturity he hadn't seen in her before, and he flashed a closed lip smile. "Thank you, Liv. I appreciate it."

As Josie slept, worry bloomed in his chest, pressing down like a heavy weight on his heart. The room, once filled with the warmth of shared dreams, now held a quiet tension. Hours passed, each one marked by the soft cadence of Josie's breaths and the intrusive ticking of the clock. In the late afternoon, Josie stirred, her eyes fluttering open as she sat up slowly. He rushed to her side, placing one hand on her leg, and one on the small of her back as he helped her lean back against the pillows.

"August? What happened?"

"You got a bit feverish after the balloon ride. Nothing to worry about, just rest," he assured, handing her a glass of water, and watching as she took a hesitant sip. "Promise me everything will be okay?" Josie whispered, her eyes searching for reassurance August took her hand in his, the promise ring glinting in the subdued light.

"I promise."

The night wore on, each passing moment etched with worry. August, unable to find solace in sleep, sat beside her, watching over her as he chewed his lip impatiently. By 2 am, exhaustion claimed him, his eyes heavy with the weight of worry. He rose from bed, splashing cool water on his face, slapping to his cheeks, and then dampening a washcloth before wringing it out. When he returned, Josie's sleep was still restless. He gently cradled her in his arms, whispering soothing words into her clammy hair, breathing cool air onto her neck, and placing the washcloth on her forehead. Soon, dawn painted the room in hues of soft pink and gold, August found himself unable to surrender to sleep's embrace. The promise of a new day carried both hope and trepidation. Josie, still nestled in a feverish slumber, appeared fragile in the early light. Liv entered the room quietly, her eyes falling upon August as he knelt beside the bed. His head was bowed, hands clasped together, elbows resting on the mattress.

"Hey, how is she? Were you up all night with her?"

August nodded his head, his voice a hushed murmur. "I don't know, Liv. She's a lot hotter than before, and she keeps tossing and turning."

"Maybe you should call a doctor."

"Yeah..." he hesitated, looking over at her as she, for once that night, lay still under the tangled blanket. "I'll look up her symptoms first, and see where to go from there."

"Okay." Liv rubbed his shoulder. "It's gonna be okay, August. I promise."

"Thanks, Liv." They exchanged a smile and Liv stood back up.

"I'll go out and grab some breakfast. Is McDonalds okay?"

"Pancakes and syrup?"

"Yep."

"Get some for Josie too. Take some cash from my wallet."

"Sure," She chuckled, leaving them alone in a silent respite. "I'll be back soon."

Chapter Fourteen

A thousand years — Christina Perri

Soft morning light danced through the curtains, casting a soft glow upon Josie as she lay in bed. The remnants of excitement from the hot air balloon adventure lingered, but beneath the surface, a thread of concern wove through the apartment. August sat down at his desk, a mug of coffee steaming upwards from his coaster, and half eaten pancakes on the side. He meticulously scrolled through pages on his laptop, worrying his bottom lip between his teeth, his eyebrows furrowed. The soft clicks of his keyboard mingled with the gentle hum of the room and the distant tick of the wall clock, creating an atmosphere of quiet determination. He read about symptoms, causes, and possible remedies, his forehead creasing with every new piece of information. He finally exhaled, took a sip of his coffee and slammed it onto the table, his breath laden with both realisation and resolve.

"Damn it." He whispered, running a hand through his hair. He stood up and made his way to the bedroom, sitting on the mattress beside her. Exhaling again, he gently nudged her awake, his eyes softening as she stirred.

"Good morning, eejit."

"Morning Liv brought breakfast for you on the table. She had to run an errand, but she'll be back soon."

She rubbed the sleep from her eyes, and smiled weakly. "You're spoiling me."

August returned the smile but a shadow lingered in his gaze. "Listen, I think you might have pneumonia. I'm going to get you some tablets to help. Will you be okay on your own for half an hour?"

"Pneumonia? Is it serious?"

August paused, his eyes falling to his hands, entwined with Josie's fingers. The air hung heavy with a weighty silence before he finally spoke. "Well, i-it's a respiratory infection, so yes."

Josie's eyes widened with worry. They glistened, reflecting the vulnerability that had settled into the room, and she clutched the blanket tighter around her, seeking comfort from its familiar warmth. A soft tremor laced her voice as she darted her eyes between his, her breath wheezy. "Will I die?"

A lump grew in his throat, aching at the raw honesty in her question. He turned to meet her gaze, the depth of her large, questioning eyes pulling at his heart. Tears tracked down her face, and he quickly moved his thumb to her face to wipe them away.

"Well," he began, his tone gentle, "you *could*, but it's not going to come to that."

"Do you promise?"

He looked across the room, listening to the drone of the cars outside for a moment, desperate to gather his scattered thoughts.

"I don't want to upset you."

"Tell me the truth." She whispered, pleading with him.

He exhaled, moving his hand to the nape of his neck. "The truth is, we're going to do everything we can to make sure that doesn't happen. I promise you, I won't let you face this alone. We'll fight this together, okay? Do you trust me?"

"I trust you. I've always trusted you."

He smiled, tears gathering in his eyes as he placed his hands on her face and kissed the top of her head.

"I'll be back in a minute." Soon, he returned with a glass of water and the knitted blanket, carefully tucking her in.

"I'm going to the pharmacy to get you some amoxicillin. It's an antibiotic. You're not allergic to penicillin, are you?"

"I don't know. What is it?"

August chuckled softly, "Oh, right, it's after your time." He placed the glass of water on the bedside table and gently touched her cheek. "Liv should be back soon, but I'll leave my phone here. Call her if you need her. You remember how to do that, hm?"

"Yes, of course."

"I'll be back soon. Enjoy your food. I love you eejit."

"I love you too, eejit!" She moved the pancakes in front of her and began to eat.

As August drove to the pharmacy, his mind churned with worry. Thoughts of Josie facing the icy aftermath of the *Titanic's* sinking lingered, and he couldn't shake the thought that the harsh conditions might be haunting her health now.

"Please, let her get better," he murmured to himself, the words a quiet plea against the backdrop of the engine's hum. He parked the car and got out, shoving his hands into his pockets.

***

"I'm sorry, Mr. Quinn, but antibiotics require a prescription. Could you possibly schedule an appointment for her to be examined?" The pharmacist's voice held a clinical but sympathetic tone.

"Please, I can't let her die. Can't I just take something for her?" August pleaded, desperation woven into his words. "Anything."

The pharmacist sighed, her expression sympathetic but firm. "There's nothing I can provide over the counter. I'm sorry."

August's frustration boiled over. He closed his eyes, and counted the pulse in his ears, slamming the counter and leaving the pharmacy. Frustration gnawed at him as he drove back home, a determined resolve settling over him as he sought a solution for Josie's growing discomfort. He took the lift, back up to the fifteenth floor, his head in his hands as he scrambled for a solution. The doors opened and he sauntered to his front door, unlocking the door and making a beeline for his room.

"Hey, what did they say?" His eyes remained void, his breathing shallow as he scooped Josie into his arms, her blanket draped around her body.

"Woah! Hey, what are you doing? Is it that serious you have to carry me to the living room?"

He carefully carried her to the sofa, and he settled her down, draping her legs over his. His expression was solemn, his eyes reflecting the weight of his concern. He reached out, taking Josie's hand in his, a silent gesture of support and reassurance amidst the uncertainty.

"What did the doctor say? Did you get the tablets for her?"

"No. You need to be prescribed these antibiotics after a fucking appointment. I tried to get them, but it's not that simple."

Her eyes reflected a mix of fear and uncertainty. "Appointment? I don't know, August. I'm scared. They'll find out I'm not from this time... they'll—"

He turned his body to face her, holding her hand, his anger disappearing. "Josie, it's the best way to help you get better. Please, think about it. I'll be right here with you."

"They'll want to test me."

"No they won't." Liv smiled, stroking her hair back. "They have a duty of care and cannot do anything without your consent. Have an appointment, get antibiotics, and that will be that."

Feeling the warmth spreading through her, Josie suddenly felt too hot. She sighed, fanning herself with her hand. "Fine. I'll have an appointment. And my hair. It's bothering me. Can you tie it back?"

August smiled, a gentle reassurance. "Of course." He gathered her hair into a loose bun, securing it with a hair tie. Josie's eyes met his, gratitude shining in them. She settled back into the sofa, a subtle cough emerging. "Thank you, August."

He brushed a loose strand of hair from her face, standing up to follow Liv to the kitchen.

"Rest, Josie. I'm going to call the doctor for an appointment."

Chapter Fifteen

Iris – The Goo Goo Dolls.

August stirred from his uneasy sleep, the haunting refrain weaving through his subconscious and pulling him into a reluctant wakefulness. The dim light unveiled Josie, her silhouette adorned with fragility. His heart echoed the irregular rhythm of her coughs, and he couldn't escape the creeping tendrils of fear that gripped him. With a tender touch, he reached out, his hand gravitating to her forehead. As his fingers brushed against her fevered skin, fear coiled in the pit of his stomach. The dawn, instead of casting a hopeful glow, amplified the shadows of his fear, a silent acknowledgment of the uncertain terrain they now navigated.

"Oh, Josie." He whispered, brushing her hair away from her forehead. Fear etched shadows on his face as he retrieved the thermometer from the bedside drawer in the dim light. The small device felt weighty in his hands, an unwelcome sign of truths he was reluctant to face. Turning back to Josie, he pressed the button, and the digital screen flickered to life. As the thermometer climbed, each digit a stark confirmation of the battle they faced, the room, once filled with shared laughter, now stood witness to a silent struggle against an invisible adversary. His gaze lingered on the numbers, their pale glow reflecting the reality that now hung in the air.

"102?" He exclaimed. "Shit!"

"Hmm... What's 102?" She murmured, stirring awake.

"Your temperature!" He swallowed, pushing his hand back into his hair as she furrowed her brow and cocked her head at him. "Oh, it's um, 39 degrees celsius."

"T-that's a bit high, isn't it?"

"Yes." He turned to face Josie, her silhouette outlined by the dim light. Her eyes, the colour of a stormy sea, met his with a vulnerability that mirrored the tentative glow of dawn. His touch sought solace on her forehead, feeling not only the warmth that betrayed the fever within but also the palpable fear that emanated from her. Her lips parted with ragged breath as he watched her. "Listen, we need to see a doctor. That cough of yours isn't letting up." he declared, his voice carrying the weight of determination and the quiet undercurrent of worry that bound them together. Her eyes, once filled with a spark of curiosity and wonder, now reflected the shadows of fear that danced in the room. "But August, what if they won't treat me? They'll want to run all sorts of tests and I don't fancy myself as the subject of them."

August's gaze softened, his thumb gently brushing a strand of hair from her face. "They won't. Do you remember what Liv said? They have a duty of care, no matter if you're 19 or 130. I just need you well again. *Please.*"

"I'm just scared. It could get out onto that... media thing you were telling me about. Millions—billions of people could find out, and you could—"

He gently pressed a kiss to her lips, a tender caress that conveyed both reassurance and a silent plea. Pulling away, he hovered over her face, their tearful eyes locking in an unspoken exchange. Shaky breaths escaped their lips in the charged atmosphere. "You could get in trouble."

"In trouble for what? Looking after you? Look, I don't care about what happens to me. I just need you to get better." The words hung in the air, heavy with the weight of love and vulnerability. "I love you so much."

The morning unfolded with a hesitant rhythm, the weight of shared laughter and quiet moments accentuating their steps. They traversed the sterile halls of the doctor's office and the walls seemed to close in, amplifying the whispers of their fears. Josie's steps were tentative and she clung to August, finding reassurance in the solid presence of his love.

"Tell me I'll be okay." She breathed, her eyes flickering across his face.

"You'll be fine, sweetheart." He squeezed her hand and pushed open the door. The scent of antiseptic and the muffled cadence of medical professionals enveloped them as they entered the doctor's office. Josie's eyes flickered with trepidation, and she hesitated at the threshold, fear casting shadows across her features. Her heart thumped as she took in the sight. A bed, a laptop, a stethoscope around the doctors neck and—

"Good morning, Josephine. I'm Doctor Carter. Call me Jade. What can we do for you today?"

Jade's warm and comforting voice filled the room, a gentle reassurance amid the clinical setting. August, seated beside Josie, watched as the examination began, the air thick with the anticipation of answers and the unspoken fears that lingered. Jade moved with a blend of clinical precision and tender care, her expertise evident in every gesture. August's gaze remained fixed on Josie, their silent exchange reflecting a shared burden of worry.

"So, it seems that you have aspiration pneumonia, Josephine. It can be caused when you inhale anything other than air into your respiratory tract. Do you have any idea of what it could be?"

Josie's eyes widened, a torrent of emotions cascading through her. Fear and uncertainty painted her gaze as she hesitated. "I-I don't know if I can say."

"Anything you say here is confidential," Jade reassured, smiling as she twirled her pen across the top of her paper. "I cannot tell anyone unless it is a harm to you or others."

"August?" She whispered, searching his face for reassurance. He smiled, a bittersweet affirmation of their shared truth.

"It's okay, tell her." He forced a smile, squeezing her hand.

"I, um, I'm actually not nineteen."

"Really? You look great for your age then." Jade attempted a light moment, crossing one leg over the other and leaning forward. "How old are you?"

"I was born in 1894. I'm 130."

"Oh. Right." Jade's eyebrows furrowed together. "So, what could've caused it then?"

Josie looked down, tears brimming in her eyes. "In 1912, I was... you've heard of *Titanic*, haven't you?"

"I think everyone who has heard of Kate Winslet has." Jade joked, laughing awkwardly at her own joke as August shot her a disapproving look.

"Who?"

"She's an actress in— never mind. Just keep going. You're doing great."

"Well, I jumped into the water when she was going down. I only had a life jacket on and a thin nightdress and it was... it was freezing, like someone was stabbing me from all over. I was all alone in the ocean. The lights were fading and the screams were blurring. I couldn't swim. I couldn't—" A choked sob escaped her as her throat tightened, memories flooding back. Water pushed down her throat, and she gasped for air, yearning for a ship to take her to safety. "Sorry. I must have... died or something. I woke up in the hospital after August found me."

"Where?"

"Ballona Creek. Near Marina Del Rey. How can we get her better?" August asked impatiently.

"Can I speak to you outside?"

He nodded, cupping Josie's face and kissing her forehead. "I'll be back in a minute."

Jade pulled the door closed, leaving Josie to absorb the information amidst medical posters.

"Listen... the thing is, Mr Quinn, her pneumonia has been left untreated for so long that..."

"You can't do anything for her," August finished, looking down, biting his lip. The truth hung heavily in the air, a suffocating acknowledgment of their reality.

"So this is it? She's going to die whether you give her the damn medicine or not?"

"I'm sorry. I'll give her a prescription to collect some antibiotics."

"Oh, what's the point? She's terminal, for god's sake!" He slammed his fist against the wall, his teeth gritting, as he attempted to breathe himself back to normal.

"Mr Quinn—"

"They said she was healthy! Why did they let her go untreated?"

"Well it's a condition that develops over time, so it may not have developed yet."

"Oh. Right. Listen, I'm sorry. H-how long does she have?"

"Do you really want to know?"

"I *need* to know." He glared at her, his eyebrows raised.

Jade exhaled, the weight of the truth crushing her spirit. "About two weeks."

"At least?"

"At most." The words hung in the air, and he raised his eyebrows, swallowing as he stared at her, all the wind knocked from his chest.

"Shit." He pressed a hand to the wall and pushed his hand back with the other. "I'm not going to tell her, Jade. I don't want her to worry. "

"I have a duty to inform the patient that—"

"*No.* I don't want her to know. Please don't tell her. *Please.*"

She exhaled, looking nervously around the room. "There's one more thing."

"What is it?"

"She also displays many symptoms of Chrono Eternal Anomaly Syndrome, or CEAS."

He frowned, leaning back against the wall. "They mentioned that. What is it?"

"It's a condition which means Josie's body doesn't age like it should. Your cells and functions stay the same over time, which is why you look and feel much younger than you should. But it also weakens your immune system, and makes you more susceptible to things like pneumonia, which sadly can be... fatal."

August's heart clenched at Jade's words, a wave of fear washing over him.

"Right. So there's absolutely *nothing* we can do to help?"

Jade shook her head. "I'm sorry, Mr Quinn. I wish I could say there was."

He walked back in the room and embraced Josie tightly, determined to make every moment count. Jade stood in the doorway, writing the words "Terminal" on her piece of paper.

"You're going to be just fine, Josie. Ja— Doctor Carter's going to prescribe you some antibiotics."

"So I won't die?"

August and Jade exchanged a knowing glance over Josie's shoulder. He shook his head, rubbing her back. "No, Josie. You're going to get better."

"You promise?"

He swallowed. "I promise."

The rest of the day unfurled in a delicate dance, a choreography of mundane rituals intertwined with profound moments. The scent of their take away dinner blended with the sea breeze on Santa Monica Pier, becoming a communion of flavours and unspoken sentiments. August, though immersed in the simplicity of the moment, couldn't escape the haunting pang of sorrow, realising that time was ephemeral. He held onto her hand as she swung her legs over the edge of the pier. *Nothing was timeless, not even her.*

"I don't know what I'd do without you, Josie."

"You'll never have to find out." Josie beamed, her hair billowing in the warm breeze. "I'm going to get better."

"I know." His voice wobbled as he drew her closer. "Thank God."

The journey continued to the beach, the waves playing a soothing melody against the shore. Josie, despite the weakness trembling through her body, ventured into the gentle ripples, a fleeting dance of carefree joy. August's eyes glistened with tears as he observed from the shore. The sand beneath his feet

became an anchor, grounding him in the present, and the realisation struck him
— he needed to embrace the moment. With a resolve etched in every step, he
slipped off his shoes and joined her in the waves. Their laughter, a harmonious
echo against the sea's backdrop, intertwined with the rhythm of the waves.
He held her close, the weight of the present moment palpable. The sun was a
golden orb painting the sky in warm hues, casting its glow over the shore, and
illuminating the love that radiated between them.

"Josie, don't exert yourself too much," he urged, his concern etching delicate
lines on his features.

"Can I swim?" she asked.

August hesitated, a canvas of worry and love playing across his gaze. "It's too
risky... if you want to get better quicker, that is."

She smiled, a bittersweet understanding passing between them. "Alright. Ice
cream and sunset, then?"

August nodded, his heart heavy with the awareness that each passing moment
brought them closer to an inevitable farewell. He watched her walk about a
foot away and then moved his hand out to hers.

"Wait." He reeled her back towards him, moving one hand to the nape of
her neck, and one hand to her waist, smiling softly as they made eye contact.
"Dance with me, then we'll get ice-cream.

"Dance with you?" Josie countered, her eyebrow raised. "We don't have any
music."

"We have the sounds of the sea and the wind, and each other. That's all we
need."

In the realm of memory and dreams, they danced. Their movements were as
light as whispers, ethereal and weightless, floating upon the currents of emotion
that bound them together. Her giggles were quiet as he spun her, the pleats
of her dress twirling in the wind. Their dance was a delicate tapestry woven
from threads of joy, sadness, and the sweet ache of love. Time stood still as they
moved, taking in the sight of the myriad of colours splayed before them in the
canvas of the sky.

"How do you feel?" He whispered, intertwining their fingers as the sun
descended below the horizon, casting a warm glow over the sand.

"Like I'm in a dream," she whispered back. "A dream I never want to end."

He smiled sadly, wrapping his arms tighter around her waist and spinning her slowly. "Dreams never end, they just evolve."

Reluctantly, they brought their dance to a graceful halt, their movements slowing like the fading echoes of a cherished melody. With a tender smile, August gently guided Josie towards the nearby ice cream stand, their fingers intertwined in a silent promise of shared moments yet to come. As they approached, the tantalising aroma of freshly churned ice cream filled the air, heightening their anticipation. With cones in hand, they found a secluded spot by the shore, the gentle lull of the waves providing a soothing backdrop to their sweet indulgence. As they savoured each bite, their laughter mingled with the soft whispers of the sea, creating a symphony of joy that echoed in their hearts long after the last traces of ice cream had melted away. The ice cream was sweet on their tongues, and melted into the symphony of the ethereal sunset. The sky, painted in hues of pink and gold, illuminated their eyes as they sat together, their bodies entwined. In the quiet lull of the evening, they found solace in each other's company. Josie's fingers traced intricate patterns in the sand, a silent acknowledgment of the fleeting nature of time. August, his gaze fixed on the horizon, experienced a delicate dance of gratitude and heartache.

"I love you, Josie," he whispered, the words a delicate murmur carried away by the sea breeze. "I always will."

She turned to him, her eyes reflecting the colours of the sunset. "And I love you, August."

The waves continued their rhythmic dance, a symphony of existence echoing the beauty of a shared journey, no matter how brief.

Chapter Sixteen

Edelweiss – Bill Lee, Charmaine Carr

"She's getting sicker," August confided, his words a reluctant admission. He cast a longing glance at Josie, her frail form a stark contrast to the memories of her vibrant self. "I-I don't think she has long left, Liv. I can't lose her."

"You won't lose her. Is the medicine not working?"

August sighed, the weight of the truth settling heavily on his shoulders. "If it was, I wouldn't be saying she's getting sicker, would I?"

A heavy pause hung in the air, the unsaid words a collective ache. Liv grappled for words that could bridge the distance and offer solace, and opened her mouth and closed it again, looking down into her lap. "Sorry, what can I do?"

August, his eyes fixed on Josie, sought solace in the connection formed by shared sorrows. He ran his fingers through her hair, careful not to wake her up. "Come over. Spend time with her before we lose her. I want to give her the best life with us."

"Okay," she replied, the unspoken promise of solidarity in her voice. "I'll be right there. Do you want me to bring anything?"

August hesitated for a moment. "Nope. Just yourself... and maybe some baking things, if you have any." As the call ended, August gently placed the phone on the bedside table, his eyes lingering on Josie's peaceful face. He cradled her with a tenderness that bordered on reverence, his fingers tracing the contours of her face, etching the memory into his heart. The weight of impending loss pressed upon him, the room filled with a quiet desperation to make every moment count.

"Don't leave me, eejit."

***

That afternoon, the kitchen became alive with the soft hum of conversation and the gentle clinking of utensils, a melody that underscored the bittersweet symphony of the moment. August's hands trembled as he reached for his phone on the countertop.

"L-let me just look up the recipe to make sure we've got everything right," he suggested, a touch of uncertainty in his voice. "Barmbrack isn't it?"

Josie shook her head with a tender smile. "August, I know this recipe like the back of my hand. My mother used to make it for us every Sunday."

"Alright then, *maestro*. Show us how it's done."

"Yes, I will!" She exclaimed, rolling up her sleeves. "It's really not hard to make."

"Oh yeah, if you actually have *some* baking ability." Liv laughed. "This one couldn't get into the Great British Bake Off if he had a robot baking with him."

"A what?"

"Robot. It's a machine which can replace humans to do things... automatically." Liv explained. "Wow, August, you've not shown her a lot, have you?" Liv's raised eyebrows betrayed mock disappointment. August scoffed, taking the bag of flour, and with a mischievous grin, he sent a flour tornado soaring through the air, and laughed as it landed on Liv's face. Caught between surprise and laughter, Liv looked at August with a mix of amusement and disbelief. "Well, that's one way to prove a point."

August, his face adorned with a self-satisfied grin, shrugged. "Hey, if you can't bake well, at least you can make a mess spectacularly, right?"

The kitchen, now dusted with a fine layer of flour, bore witness to a culinary showdown that had unexpectedly veered into the realm of hilarity. Josie, caught in the crossfire of kitchen antics, joined in the laughter, her eyes sparkling with the absurdity of the floury spectacle.

"Right, come on you eejits. Do you want brack today or not?"

"What even is it?" Liv asked.

"It's a type of bread with sultanas and raisins. At Halloween, we put something inside it, and whoever gets it is supposed to be lucky."

"Oh, so like La Galette des Rois en France?"

"*Similare, oui*. I spent January in France once and had *une galette des rois*. That year, my father got the trinket, la fève[1], and that was the year he got a job at Harland and Wolff."

"Wow, that's amazing." August exclaimed.

"Yes. I wonder if he continued working at the shipyard after Titanic."

---

1. https://en.wikipedia.org/wiki/F%C3%A8ve

"We can find out."

"Really? Can we? Now?"

"When we've finished, yes."

Josie nodded, and they continued their dance around the kitchen, each movement imbued with a profound sense of purpose. Josie's hands guided Liv and August through the nuances of the recipe—the careful folding of ingredients, the rhythmic stirring, the precise measurement of spices.

"W-wait! One last secret ingredient!" She stood up and slowly moved towards the spice rack. "Nutmeg. Just a sprinkle. You'll need to grate it."

As the scent of Barmbrack wafted through the kitchen, August couldn't help but steal glances at Josie. Her eyes, once bright with vivacity, now held a poignant wisdom, a reflection of a life well-lived. Liv, sensing the gravity of the moment, exchanged a knowing look with August. There was an unspoken agreement that this, this shared endeavour, was a sacred act of love.

Josie, her movements becoming more deliberate, eased into a chair. "I used to sit, just like this, while my mother worked her magic. She'd tell me stories of her youth, of love and loss, all woven into the folds of this very recipe. And nutmeg was the secret touch, the ingredient that made it uniquely ours."

August nodded, his fingers deftly grating the nutmeg, each turn of the greater releasing an aromatic cloud that wrapped around them like a comforting embrace. Josie continued, her voice a soothing cadence. "It's funny how certain scents can transport you, isn't it? The moment I took the nutmeg out, I'm back in Belfast surrounded by the laughter of my family."

August, his gaze fixed on the mixing bowl, replied, "Scents are like time travellers, Josie. They take us back to moments we thought we'd lost. And in this kitchen, right now, it feels like we're living in a beautiful, fragile bubble of time."

Josie's eyes softened with gratitude. "You've always had a way with words, August. A poet's soul, that's what you've got."

The Barmbrack, now moulded into shape, went into the oven—a vessel of memories poised to transform in the crucible of heat. As they waited, August moved to his laptop, his eyes narrow as he hunched over in an attempt to focus. "Was Barmbrack your go-to dessert, then?"

Josie chuckled, a sound that resonated with a lifetime of stories. "Oh, no. It was reserved for special occasions, moments when we needed a taste of comfort.

My mother used to say that life is too short not to indulge in the sweet things, especially when faced with the bitter."

"I just looked up your parents, Josie."

"What happened to them?" She drew closer to the laptop screen. "Michael Melrose stopped working at the Harland and Wolff shipyard after the sinking of the *Titanic* to grieve his daughter, Josephine who died on board. He later opened a blacksmithing forge to keep working on his skills he had when building ships. In 1947, following a heart attack, Michael died. He was buried in Belfast. Meanwhile his wife, Roísín, never stopped grieving. She turned into herself for a few years and didn't want anything to do with Belfast or the shipyards. In 1914 with the outbreak of war she landed a job as a nurse in London, and stayed on after the war. She never returned to Belfast, and died aged 80 in 1954 peacefully in her sleep." She paused, her eyes brimming with tears, and she swallowed the lump in her throat.

The oven timer chimed, snapping them out of their reverie. The Barmbrack, golden and inviting, beckoned from the oven. Josie wiped the tears from her eyes and moved towards the oven.

"It's ready," she declared, a shaky triumphant note in her voice.

"Josie, are you okay? I'm sorry I showed you that."

"No, I wanted to know." She smiled, bringing the barmbrack to the table, three plates in her other hand. "I'm happy I know."

They gathered around the table, the warmth of the baked pudding filling the air. August, cutting slices with a careful precision, felt the weight of the moment settle around them like a soft shroud. The first bites were a communion of flavours and memories, a communion of past and present.

"To life, to love, and to the moments that linger even when we must say goodbye." As they savoured the dessert, Josie raised her glass, the Irish cider effervescing in the delicate crystal. "Sláinte," she whispered, her voice carrying a silent plea for blessings on the journey ahead. They clinked glasses, the sound echoing in the quiet kitchen. For a moment, time stood still, and in that shared toast, they acknowledged the beauty of a friendship that had weathered storms and the fragility of a life that had blossomed even in the shadow of farewell.

"Out of curiosity," Josie beamed, swallowing a mouthful of cider. "How many languages do you know how to say cheers in?"

"Five."

"Five!? Go on then," Josie prodded, her smile widening.

"Cheers, sláinte, santé, prost, skál."

"And which languages are they?" Josie inquired, her interest piqued.

"English, Irish, French, German, and Icelandic. I like..."

"Learning!" Liv and Josie exclaimed simultaneously, their voices perfectly in sync, sealing their shared enthusiasm with a high-five.

"Showoff."

"Is that the only word you know?" August countered, bringing the glass to his lips and laughing silently. Unable to resist the playful tease, Liv playfully hit him on the arm.

"I'm gonna miss this."

"Why would you miss it?" Josie whispered, her eyebrows raised. "I'm getting better, aren't I?"

"Sometimes missing something is a way of holding onto what we fear losing the most."

"That doesn't tell me anything." Her eyes widened, pleading with him.

"I'm sorry." August's fingers clenched around her hand, the warmth of their connection tinged with an underlying tremor. His gaze, a silent plea, met Liv's in a fleeting moment of shared worry. The room held its breath as August continued, "I just don't want to lose you. Life is so ephemeral... so unpredictable."

"Maybe, but you won't lose me." She reassured, placing her hands on either side of his neck and kissing his forehead. "I'm getting better. Right?"

Chapter Seventeen

Hand to hold– JJ Heller

The room was cloaked in shadows, the dim light revealing the contours of despair etched on August's face. His eyes were once bright with hope, but now mirrored the sombre gravity of the moment. Beside him, Josie lay in a fitful sleep, oblivious to the tempest of emotions swirling within him. August sat hunched over by the bedside, the sound of her increasingly laboured breathing punctuating the oppressive silence. The night air hung heavy with unspoken grief, the weight of an unfulfilled promise etched across August's features.

Beside him, a crystal-clear glass sat on the nightstand, and with trembling hands, August poured a measure of amber liquid into it. He hesitated, his fingers lingering on the glass—a silent admission of defeat. It was a drink he vowed never to touch, a promise made to Liv: a promise he couldn't keep.

"You said you'd never drink." Liv whispered, holding his hand. His eyes turned to hers, softening as a tear slipped hesitantly from the corner.

"I can't not. This is too much, Liv. I'm sorry." As the liquid swirled in the glass, August's mind replayed the moments that led him to this point. He recalled Jade's clinical words, the hushed conversation in the hallway, and the haunting images of Josie's weakening frame each night. He had promised himself he wouldn't be here again—watching a loved one slip away, helpless to intervene. Turning his gaze to Liv, August whispered in the darkened room, "I can't, Liv. I can't watch her fade away. Not again."

"This is about mom isn't it?" She gripped the glass, attempting to pry it from his hands. "August, you can't compare mom's death to Josie's illness. And you shouldn't turn yourself into dad turning to alcohol."

"I'm not."

Liv widened her eyes and gestured to the glass in his hands.

"That's one drink, it's hardly descending into alcoholism. It's just...Seeing her like this. It feels like I'm holding my breath until she's better. But knowing she's not going to... to get better. I mean I might as well be suffocating, Liv."

"You promised me you wouldn't do that to yourself. We promised we'd face whatever life throws at us together."

August's eyes flickered with a mixture of pain and resignation as he nodded in agreement, swallowing the lump in his throat. "Promises can't always be kept. It's just one drink."

He held the glass to his lips and stared at Liv, watching her eyes droop with discontent.

"You can't let the fear of losing her paralyse you. We have each other, August. Promise me you won't shut yourself off."

August took a deep breath, his shoulders tensing against the weight of Liv's words. He met her gaze, a storm of conflicting emotions swirling in his eyes. "I know, Liv. But this... this is different. I can't lose her. I can't. I might as well be dead without her."

"Don't say that, August."

"Josie is my whole world, Liv!" He whisper yelled, slamming a hand on the mattress. "She's my whole world, my whole universe. She's shown me how beautiful the world is again, how much the little moments matter! If she dies... I will die with her."

August took a shaky breath, his resolve crumbling like ancient parchment. The glass met his lips, the bitter liquid a stark contrast to the sweetness of memories he sought to preserve. Liv sighed as the bitter liquid flowed into his mouth, a stark contrast to the sweetness of the memories they once shared. It was a sound born from the depths of her emotions, a mix of frustration, hurt, and a touch of resignation. She shook her head, the disappointment in her eyes palpable as her gaze fixed on August with a mixture of disbelief and sorrow. Josie stirred in her sleep, her frail form a reminder of the fragility of life. Her eyes fluttered open and she glowered at August.

"You're drinking, it must be bad. How long do I have left to live?"

August hesitated, a surge of emotion burning his throat. "Rest, Josie. You need to rest."

"No! Tell me! Jade didn't, and neither did you. I don't want to be left out of the loop anymore! Please."

His gaze fell to the floor, the weight of his words a heavy burden. He put the glass on the nightstand and pushed a hand down his face, blinking slowly. "A-about a week."

Fear flashed in Josie's eyes, and her mouth dropped, her voice quivering as she spoke, "A week? You *knew*, and you didn't tell me? Why? Is that why Jade took you outside? You promised I wouldn't die, August. You lied to me!"

August felt the sting of her words, each syllable a dagger piercing his heart. He reached out, wiping away Josie's tears, his own falling freely, and held her wrists gently. "It's the only promise I can't keep, Josie. I'm sorry. I didn't mean to lie to you. I was—"

"He wanted you to enjoy life without that burden." Liv explained, extending a shaky hand to Josie's arm. "Don't be too hard on him."

"I don't want to die again, August. I'm scared."

"I know you are. I am too." His hands trembled as he reached over to her shoulders. "I-Have a song you might like to listen to, it's helping me sort out my emotions. I might help you too"

"Is it in our playlist?"

"If you want it to be." He whispered, his voice choked as the gentle piano melody weaved through the room. The notes hung in the air like a fragile thread connecting their hearts.

"What's it called?"

"Hand to hold, JJ Heller."

"Put it in the playlist."

He nodded, watching tears stain her face as he turned his phone off and placed it on the pillow behind him. A tangible tension settled between them, suffusing the air with unspoken emotions. The atmosphere grew heavy with the weight of impending loss, and August's trembling hands remained cradling Josie's hands, an anchor in the sea of uncertainties. Their soft breathing and sniffles synchronised with the slow, melancholic piano notes, each shaky inhale and exhale resonating with the shared fear and sorrow that hung between them. The room became a sanctuary of quiet anguish, the only sound the gentle rise and fall of their breaths. Tears welled in Josie's eyes, glistening like dewdrops on fragile petals. August, too, fought back the tears that threatened to spill over. Silent sobs escaped them, an intimate duet blending with the melancholy tune. The music wrapped around them like a shroud, weaving an ethereal connection that transcended words.August's fingers traced delicate patterns on Josie's reddening cheeks, catching the tear trails as they made their way down. As the final notes of the song lingered, the room held onto the echoes of their shared grief. August moved his hands to her face, wiping the residue of their tears staining the fabric of their souls.

"Josie, sweetheart," he began, his voice a delicate cadence in the solemn room, "you don't have long. Life can be cruel, but it can also be beautiful, filled with little things that make us feel happy. Like puddles, ships, and planes, movie days, music, and sunset dreams with ice-cream. You're the best dream I will ever dream, the best song I will ever hear. You will always have my hand to hold. I promise."

"You're still so poetic, August. Never lose that."

August laughed, wrapping an arm around her waist, and leaning into her.

"I have one question though."

"What's that?"

"You promised I wouldn't die. Why can't you promise now?"

He took a deep breath, the weight of his words lingering in the air. "I can't promise what I can't control. I can only promise to be here, to hold your hand until the very end."

"I won't get to be an art teacher." Josie hung her head, the weight of unrealised dreams casting a shadow over her. "Tell Lea I'm sorry for disappointing her. And I'm sorry I've disappointed you."

August reached for her hand, gently lifting her chin to meet his gaze. "Hey, you haven't disappointed anyone, okay? Your journey has been extraordinary. I'm so proud of the woman you've become and all that you've accomplished. Being with you has been one of the greatest joys of my life, and I'll never forget you, *ever*. You've shown me the simple beauties in life, the things we overlook because we're used to them. You helped me see the magic again"

"The magic was always there, August. I just helped you remember how to look." She forced a smile, wrapping her arms around his shoulders. "I'll miss you, August"

His eyes softened, taking in her tear stained cheeks, her bluish lips, and eyes that had cradled the world's reflections for over a century, holding within their gaze a silent poetry.

"I'll miss you too, Josephine."

Chapter Eighteen

Timeless – Taylor Swift.

The night air cradled August and Josie in its cool embrace as he gently lifted her into his arms, her legs draped over his forearm. The soft glow of the streetlights painted a cityscape that shimmered with an ethereal allure, and the warmth of a cosy blanket enveloped her shoulders, a comforting cocoon against the crispness of the evening breeze. Cradling her carefully, he carried her towards the car, settling her into the passenger seat, and clipping her seatbelt in. Her eyes grew heavy with the weight of the day, conveying a weariness that seeped into the fabric of her soul. The car's engine hummed to life, and the rhythmic purr merged seamlessly with the gentle lull of the vehicle, coaxing Josie into a drowsy state.

"Stay awake, sweetheart," August implored, the urgency in his voice blending with the tenderness that filled the air. Fingers deftly danced over the music console, selecting an upbeat tune that resonated through the car. Its lively rhythm, a spirited attempt to anchor Josie in wakefulness, mingled with the night's serenade. Yet, despite August's efforts, the magnetic pull of sleep tugged at her. Nestled within the blanket's warmth, she found herself surrendering to the night's lullaby, her eyelids fluttering closed. August stole glances at her delicate silhouette.

"Play the car song, mo ghile mear." Josie drawled. "I need to hear it again."

A soft smile graced August's lips as he reached for the playlist, finding "Bitter Sweet Symphony" and allowing its familiar, comforting melody to fill the car. The first chords resonated, the air in the car shifted, and the comforting melody wrapped around them like a warm embrace. The subtle dance of emotions played across August's face.

"Turn it up. Deafen me with music."

August's eyes, already softened, glinted with a mixture of understanding and heartache. Without a word, he reached for the volume knob, turning it up gradually. The melody, once a gentle hum, now surged with newfound intensity, filling the car's confines. As the music enveloped them, August stole glances at Josie, observing the subtle shifts in her expression as the sound surrounded her. There was a reverence in his actions, a silent acknowledgment of the power of their playlist. The air in the car became charged with emotions, and for a moment, the outside world ceased to exist, leaving only the pulsating beats and the echoes of a life lived fully. Winding through the secluded roads, the car song enveloped them in a shared moment of solace. August's gaze lingered on Josie, her eyes closed, lost in the tender embrace of the music.

"Hey, Josie, I found this new song. It's called 'Timeless.' It's about us." His voice wavered, a raw vulnerability laid bare in the intimate space between them. The opening guitar chords filled the car, wrapping around them like a tender embrace. August's eyes held Josie's, the weight of the lyrics sinking into the quiet, sacred space they occupied.

"Music will always remind me of you." He smiled, rubbing the pad of his thumb over the back of her hand.

"Why?"

"Because every song carries the imprint of our moments together," August's voice shook as he breathed slowly. "You've become the soundtrack to my life, a-and every time music plays, it's like hearing the echoes of us – the laughter, the quiet moments, the shared dreams. Music is our memories. Music is timeless. Just like you. Just like us."

A tremulous smile played on her lips as she leaned on his shoulder, the gentle rub of August's thumb on the back of her hand grounding her.

"We really were timeless, weren't we?" Her gaze lingered on August's, and in that silent exchange.

Time paused as the Hollywood hills cradled their journey, and the music painted the canvas of
their history.

"Come on, we're here. Do you want to walk?"

She nodded, and he guided her out of the car, his arm around her waist. But as her feet met the ground, an unexpected weakness overcame her, and her knees buckled. Reacting with a swift and steady strength, he scooped her up into his arms, cradling her delicately against him.

"I'm sorry. I wanted to— by myself."

"I know you did, sweetheart. I don't mind carrying you though."

She let her head drop back onto his arm. "What's this?"

"The Hollywood sign. It was built in 1923 as an advertisement which read Hollywoodland. It was designed by an Englishman named Thomas Fisk Goff." He sat down behind the sign sitting her on his knee. The city was vast and endless around them, with lights shining from every corner, with soft purple clouds dancing in the air around them.

"Trust you to know the ins and outs of it. You *really* know everything, don't you? I like to learn because of you, and for that I'll never be able to thank you enough."

August exhaled, blinking away his tears. "You're timeless, Josephine. *Beidh grá agam duit i gcónaí." I'll always love you.*

He looked into her eyes, bringing a warm hand to her face and she tiredly leaned into it, biting her lower lip and smiling softly. He wrapped an arm around her and she leant her head on his shoulder, and closed her eyes, feeling the stubble on his face, and trying to contain a laugh at the thought of him trying to grow a beard. The night grew quieter, the sunset fading into darkness...

***

"Josie? I think it's time to go home. It's getting late." He tapped her face, her coldness seeping into his fingertips. Exhaling, he darted his eyes across the city, the lights becoming blurs setting fire to his eyes.

"Josie?" Another tap. He shook her lightly. "Come on, don't trick me. This isn't funny."

He stared down at her, brushing a strand of her hair away from her face, and looking down at her hands, noticing the emerald ring on her finger.

"Oh god." He whispered, holding a shaking hand over his mouth, defeated. "Josephine, please. Josephine! You still have a week left! No—"

He looked to the sunset, the oranges and pinks. It was smiling at him. *She is safe with us. She is painting the sunset for you.* A weak smile broke across his face and a tear succumbed and tumbled down his cheek. *She wasn't suffering anymore.* He took his phone from his jean pocket and laid her down into the grass, smoothing out her faded green t-shirt and her jeans.

A girl from 1912 should not belong, should not fit into his world, but yet she did. For a short while, she was the best part of it.

August urgently unlocked his phone and composed a message for Liv, his fingers moving swiftly across the screen: "Come to the Hollywood sign ASAP. She's gone..." He pressed send, the weight of the words hanging in the air. In a swift and decisive motion, he dialled 911 into the keypad, and brought the phone to his ear, awaiting the connection.

"Yes, ambulance please. We're at the Hollywood sign. She's painting sunsets now."

The sunset cradled Josephine's soul that evening, lifting her high above the clouds and the blinking stars. In body, she was 130 but in mind she was nineteen, exploring the world anew. 111 years later. With him. August. The man sitting on the hill overlooking Hollywood, holding the dead girl in his arms. The man who liked to learn. He loved a timeless girl, the last *Titanic* survivor and she had trusted him enough to guide her through the world, to let him love her and to love him back. August looked down, the cool autumn winds wiping his tears away. He wanted to be strong for her. *He needed to.*

The sound of his voice into the phone was enough to break him down. A lump formed in his throat as more and more tears plummeted down his cheeks. He looked down to her limp hands, to her tattoo, and held it to his face, the last of her warmth seeping into his cheeks. His breaths were ragged and uneven and he was certain his eyes could be mistaken for Niagara falls. An ambulance wailed in the background, crying with him. He looked around, watching blue lights rise up over the hill, park 75 feet behind them, and then two paramedics run in slow motion to him, followed behind by Liv.

"What happened, sir?"

"She's very ill. She wanted to make the most of the world before she died."

"What was her name?"

"Josi— Josephine Melrose."

"And how old is she?" August looked down at her and traced her cheeks, her nose and her lips with his thumb.

"130."

A soft gasp from one of the paramedics as he loaded her body onto a stretcher. He looked down at her and up at Liv, who was helping him up from the ground, the knitted blanket in hand. Josie was so young, but so old. Her skin was so soft, her hair was so red and vivacious, but her soul belonged in sepia toned photographs.

"Josie's timeless," He smiled at her one last time. "She always has been."

Liv watched his eyes as he stuffed his hand into his pocket, retrieving the box, and watching as the ambulance doors closed. His lips parted as he turned to Liv, and then back to the ambulance.

"Wait!" He jogged towards the vehicle, and opened the box, revealing an emerald-green pear-shaped gem which caught the refracted light of shared dreams.

"What is it?"

"I was going to give this to her... on her birthday. It was going to be a promise ring to her to—"

"Do you want to give it to her?" A paramedic interrupted, opening the door again. August's lips parted, tears tracking down his face as he removed the ring from the box, balancing it on his thumb, and stepping into the ambulance. He sat on the chair, taking her left hand in hers.

"Oh, Josie, you eejit. Why did you have to leave me?" He sniffed, looking down into his hand, and smiling. "I was supposed to give you this, and make a whole sappy speech. I was supposed to remind you... Ní bhaineann an t-am le muinín, ach le mothú. *Trust isn't about time, but a feeling.* A-and you were supposed to accept it as a promise to love and trust you for the rest of our lives. We were supposed to have forever." He slid the ring onto her finger, kissed her knuckles, and bowed his head, turning to leave the ambulance. "Good night, Josephine. I'll love you forever."

Each minute ticked by in slow motion, leaving behind a haunting silence that mirrored the vast void in August's heart. His lips quivered with wracked sobs, each gasp echoing the unbearable weight of a loss too profound for words. He enveloped himself, wrapping his arm around his waist, fingers clutching the edges of the blanket Liv had wrapped around him. His nose sought refuge at the top, inhaling deeply, trying to capture and hold onto her lingering scent

"Come on, let's get you home," Liv whispered, her voice a delicate thread in the tapestry of grief. They moved with a slow numbness, getting into the car where the engine hummed to life. The radio immediately turned on, its notes weaving a melancholy melody around them.

"No— Music reminds—" August's voice, fragile and strained, broke the oppressive quietude. Liv nodded, and reached to the dashboard, silencing the music. The knitted blanket, laden with shared sorrow, enveloped him, and sheltered him from a world that felt so different without her.

"Will you stay with me tonight? I don't want to be alone. I'm afraid I'll drink again, and I need to keep at least one of my promises." August cried, wiping his cheeks dry in vain.

A soft smile graced Liv's lips. "Of course. We're going to get through this together. I promise. You're not alone. You're not alone."

He nodded, feeling more hot tears track down his cheeks, his eyelids becoming heavy as he succumbed to sleep, each tear carrying the weight of a love that now existed in the realm of memories and echoes, songs, and drawings. The drone of passing cars on the road and the distant wail of sirens became the soundtrack to his heartache, a symphony of grief that played in tandem with the rhythm of the night.

It was on this summer night in Los Angeles that August Quinn learnt something brand new. Something he never went out of his way to learn, something he never wanted to have to learn.

Time leaves its mark on everyone, but within the sanctuary of your heart, the presence of the person you love defies the ticking clock, and they become timeless.

Epilogue

Songbird — Live 1977 —Fleetwood Mac
Monday, 21st August 2023

The first day back at school unfurled like a grey, unwelcome canvas for August Quinn. His shoulders sagged under the weight of a grief so palpable it had become an unwelcome companion. He was an echo of his former self. The familiar hum of the classroom, once a comforting backdrop to his lesson, now seemed discordant. He stood before the sea of faces, placing his bag on his chair and attempting to summon the enthusiasm that had defined him. He cleared his throat, grappling with a subject that had once been his solace.

"Good morning, guys. I'm Mr Quinn. I'm going to be your physics teacher for this year." He stroked his chin feeling the unwelcome hair sprouting, and scoffed. "It's going to be really fun, and you're going to learn... a lot. She *loved* to learn." He whispered the last part, lowering his gaze down to his forearm.

"Mr. Quinn, is that a tattoo?"

"What does it say?"

He glanced down at the inked words on his forearm. "Táimid gan am. It's Irish," he muttered, the words carrying the weight of a language that now felt foreign. His eyes remained cast down, and he pursed his lips, feeling sobs rise in his throat.

"Sir? Are you okay?" Another voice, tinged with concern, cut through the silence. He nodded, his eyes dark as he scanned the room.

"What does it mean?" Curiosity and whispers began to ripple through the classroom.

"It means we are timeless. I always liked to believe she was."

August found himself standing before a sea of curious faces, the weight of her death exposed. He cleared his throat and looked back up, breathing himself back to a calm state as he surveyed the teenagers in front of him. He smiled, taking the cap off a whiteboard pen.

"Right, that's enough, I don't want to talk about it anymore. We're learning about radiation today. Can anyone start us off by listing the electromagnetic spectrum?" A hand eagerly shot up and a smile painted itself onto August lips. "Go ahead."

"Radio, microwave, infrared, ultraviolet, x-ray, and gamma."

"Almost perfect! You just missed out visible light. Great job though!" His voice was confident, but his hands trembled, the invisible strings of grief controlling his body. The once ordered notes on the board seemed to blur, mirroring the chaos that had infiltrated his own thoughts.

"Sir, who was she?"

He turned around, his eyes fogged over as memories of her played back, her laughter ringing in his ears. His lips tugged into a smile as the memories played back.

"No, I think they died out when people realised breathing and moving comfortably was kind of important."

"You can put together a bunch of songs you like and call it a playlist. Then, you can listen to it whenever you want."

"I kissed you because I couldn't bear the thought of you leaving. I was scared of losing what we have, losing you."

"Dance with you? We don't have any music."

"We have the sounds of the sea and the wind, and each other. That's all we need."

"Sir?"

"Hm?"

"Who was she?" The question hung in the air, an unspoken plea for the teacher to unveil the woman who had left an indelible mark on his soul. August hesitated, his eyes momentarily searching for a lifeline amid the tumult of emotions.

"I don't think it's appropriate or relevant to the electromagnetic spectrum do you, Sara?"

"Please, sir."

He exhaled, twisting his pen lid, taking it off and putting it back on with a click. "Her name was Josie," he began, the name heavy with a weight he could not fully articulate. "She was meant to be an art teacher here." The students exchanged glances, the revelation rendering them silent witnesses to a tragedy they could scarcely comprehend. A web of curiosity and sympathy wove itself through the room, each student grappling with the realisation that their once animated teacher was now a wounded man. His face became a window into a world where joy had been replaced by sorrow. The memory of her painted strokes and dreams echoed in his words, leaving an imprint that hovered in the air like a bittersweet melody.

"She was *so* beautiful, indescribably so. She loved to learn, loved to draw, loved everything there is to love. She had a thirst for life that was... contagious."

"How did she die?"

"Jax!"

"What? I'm just curious."

"Yes, but it's insensitive."

"Aspiration pneumonia." August stated, his eyes softening. "We caught it early, but the medicine didn't help."

"Was she actually 130?"

"Yes."

"So she was born in 1893. Oh my god, she was around when the *Titanic* sank. Did you know that sir? Was she on it? Please tell us!"

The bell, a welcome interruption, peeled its 11 am break time signal. The students, their curiosity momentarily sated, scattered, leaving August alone in the classroom. The hollowness that enveloped him seemed to echo through the empty spaces. He sat down on his chair and placed his head in his hands, leaning into the table with a shaky exhale. Picking up a pen, he scribbled a note to himself on some lined paper, and then traced the inked words with trembling fingers.

"Mr Quinn, do you have a moment? I just need a word."

"Oh hey Lea, sure." He covered his forearm and sat upright, wiping the last of the tears which tracked down his face.

"What were you writing?"

"A note to Josie."

"What does it say?"

His breath caught in his throat, and he swallowed. "Even in the emptiness, your memory resonates. And in the echoes of our shared experiences, I find a timeless connection that not even the solitude of these walls can erase."

"That's beautiful. Very poetic."

He smiled, looking into Lea's eyes with a mixture of pain and admiration.

"Listen, I know what you're going through must be so hard, August. If you need some time off, just come and find me, okay. I'm always here."

"Thank you. I'll be okay. I need to get out of the house."

"Too many memories, hm?" She rubbed his shoulder, watching him look down to his feet, nodding pensively.

Closing his eyes, he pictured his fifteenth floor apartment, the lava lamp in the corner that drowned the room in syrupy lights, the small kitchen with a tub of leftover Barmbrack on the side, the half-finished packet of her antibiotics on the coffee table. He looked across to his desk, seeing his laptop with their playlist on one tab and flight tracker on the next. He walked into his room, seeing the tangled bedsheets, and the knitted blanket spread across the bed. The warmth of her arms and the smell of floral perfume drifted towards him as he leant across the mattress, plumping her pillow, and draping the blanket over her side of the bed. He walked out into the hallway, watching her face become alight with a smile, one so picture perfect it made his cheeks sprout dahlias. His trainers squeaked as he crossed the distance between them and enveloped her in his arms, pressing a kiss on her lips as she tangled her hands in his hair. He drew closer to her ear, whispering almost silently, "You're ethereal, Josie. In life and in death, we'll always be timeless."

The End.

Acknowledgements
Josephine — Applewood Road

Timeless came about from a recurring daydream I had walking home from the bus stop after college. There is an engraved stone brick at the front of an old Sunday School (now a block of flats) which says "April 14th, 1903". It wasn't the same year, but nine years before Titanic hit the iceberg. But I thought, "What would a girl do in this year if she had time-travelled from Titanic? How would she navigate the world? What if I was her?" Then I decided — it has to be a love story! Cliché, sure. A girl time travels and falls in love with the first person she meets. But it was something I kept thinking about. Josephine became a part of me even before I wrote about her, and I quickly wanted to be her as she navigated lots of things which to us are ordinary: aeroplanes, music, Julie Andrews in The Sound of Music. This curiosity, a childlike wonder, is downplayed in our everyday life. Unless we live close to an airport or purposely go plane spotting, it's a case of if we see a plane, it's just a dot in the sky. Maybe we think about the passengers or where it's going, but it's never really exciting. But for Josie, it was something so distant in the future that it's as small as it is incomprehensible. Writing Timeless has been a nice breath of air: a chance to experience life vicariously through her. I also wanted to be August: constantly learning, teaching, kindling sparks of curiosity in everyone he meets. I learnt a lot about a lot writing this book, and I enjoyed every minute of it!

Obviously, Titanic had to play a part in this book. When I watched it for the first time in lockdown, I never imagined how it would change my life. Two books, more maritime-themed books on the way, and a place at University studying Nautical Science starting in September 2024. I owe a lot to Titanic, and even if it's just in a small way, I like to think writing about her story and her passengers (albeit fictional) may give just one person a passion that changes their life like it changed mine. Once again, I'd like to use my acknowledgments space to thank the people who believed in me, in the child who incessantly told everyone she wanted to be an author, for reading parts and giving me feedback. I want to thank the Titanic community: the people who engage in discussions, post pictures and articles online, the people who write books, draw pictures, upload videos on YouTube, and keep a century-old ocean liner alive for mine, and many generations to come. I owe a lot to you all.